OTHER BOOKS BY BRADLEY BOOTH

Plagues in the Palace
The Prodigal
They Call Him the Miracle Man

SHEPHERD
WARRIOR

BRADLEY BOOTH

Pacific Press® Publishing Association
Nampa, Idaho
Oshawa, Ontario, Canada
www.pacificpress.com

Designed by Gerald Lee Monks
Cover art by Lars Justinen

Additional copies of this book are available by calling toll free
1-800-765-6955 or by visiting www.adventistbookcenter.com

Library of Congress Cataloging-in-Publication Data

Booth, Bradley, 1957-
Shepherd warrior / Bradley Booth.
p. cm.
Summary: Once again sixteen-year-old David is sent to herd the sheep and
not allowed to accompany his older brothers to fight the Philistines, but
things change when David is asked to take supplies to his brothers.
ISBN 978-0-8163-2161-2
1. David, King of Israel. 2. Goliath, (Biblical giant). 3. Bible. O.T.
—History of Biblical events. 4. Conduct of life. 5. Courage. I. Title

PZ7.B46315Sh 2007

dc22   2006052489

September 2016

DEDICATION

To my two nephews, Brian and Brendan, who love

adventure stories as much as I do.

My prayer is that this book will help you boys identify with

David, who was not afraid to stand for what's right even

though others doubted him.

CONTENTS

A Time for War

The bonfire in the courtyard crackled to life as David threw another log on its dying embers. He sat down to soak in the warmth of the flames and to rest his tired body. The hour was late, but everywhere the household was still in a bustle. Servants loaded food supplies onto two-wheeled carts, a small herd of goats milled about bleating, and children shrieked as they played their late-evening games.

David sniffed the good smells of the food being loaded onto the carts. There were rolls of cheese, baskets of fragrant, crusty barley loaves fresh out of the ovens, and sacks of parched grain. Dried fruits were also being packed—raisins, figs, and olives would keep a long time.

David could hear his mother giving last-minute instructions to the servants about preparations for the trip the next day. Their chatter kept up with their busy fingers and hands. David smiled to himself. There was always so much work in the household for women to do, but always David's mother managed to remain cheerful. And right now, staying cheerful might be a very hard thing for her to do, David realized. Tomorrow at dawn, her three oldest sons would be marching off to battle the Philistines. No one really knew how long they would be gone. David knew his mother was probably worrying herself sick at the thought.

David sighed. In some ways he wished he could go with his

brothers. He was tired of always having to stay behind. He was weary of doing all the boring jobs at home that no one else wanted to do. With so many older brothers and sisters, he would never be the boss. Not in his family, and probably not in his lifetime.

David pulled his tunic closer about him. He squinted as he picked up a stick and poked at the logs in the fire. The fire felt warm on his face as a spiral of sparks sailed up into the dark night and disappeared.

What is it like to go away and fight? David wondered. *It seems like it should be exciting, but then again, going into battle must be terribly frightening too.* When he closed his eyes, David could almost see the hundreds of enemy soldiers running toward him shouting their battle cries. He could almost hear the clang of swords on swords during ferocious fighting. He could also imagine what a battlefield would look like with the bodies of dead men lying everywhere.

David glanced across the fire at his oldest brother, Eliab, who was sharpening his sword. Eliab looked like a soldier, with his leather armored vest and his spear stuck into the ground beside him. His jet black eyes looked stern, and his jaw muscles tightened as he gripped his sword in his strong, sinewy hand. As he slid the whetstone down the full length of the blade, it looked like a deadly weapon—and heavy too. Probably not as heavy as the king's sword, though.

David's heart beat faster as he remembered the stories his brothers told every time they came home from one of their military campaigns with the king. Sometimes the stories were about long marches through desert country or climbing up rocky cliffs to take the enemy by surprise. David loved to hear about the gallant king leading his soldiers into battle while astride his noble steed. According to Abinadab, David's second-oldest brother, the king's horse was white, and there was none other like it in the entire kingdom. Strong, large, and with sinewy muscles, the horse could go all day and catch any fleeing enemy soldier anywhere in the country.

And the king was a big man, too—a head taller than any of his men. David had seen King Saul only once, and then only from a distance. It had been when David was younger, and the family had gone to the tabernacle at Nob to worship during the Passover Feast. The King had looked magnificent in his royal robes. He was handsome and strong, and to David he looked just like a king should look.

But are magnificent robes and horses what being king is all about? David wasn't sure. *Is King Saul really the leader everyone had hoped he would be?* Troubles were brewing once again in the west with the hated Philistines. Earlier in his reign, King Saul had been successful in his ongoing war with the Philistines, but lately rumors were going around that the king had turned against God. That was a scary thought. If the Lord wasn't with King Saul, could the king be trusted? And could Israel ever again win a battle without a godly man at the head of its army?

Eliab stood to his feet and ran his whetstone down the edge of the sharp blade one more time before sliding the sword into its sheath. As Eliab turned to leave, David jumped to his feet.

"Eliab?" David grinned excitedly. He was almost afraid to ask the question. "Do you think I could join the army sometime soon and fight with you and Abinadab and Shammah for the king?" David held his breath. He knew it sounded foolish, but he didn't care. Right now he was nearly bursting with pride at his three oldest brothers and their bravery in going away to fight for their country and their king. David just wanted to be with them, that's all.

Eliab turned and frowned at David. "What are you grinning about, boy? War is a serious thing! One of these days maybe you'll understand that." Eliab shook his head. "You're not old enough to fight, anyway, so you can get that notion out of your head! When you're a grown man, then you can sign up."

"But I want to go now!" blurted David, and as soon as he had said the words, he wished that he hadn't. He knew it made him sound like a child.

"Nonsense!" Eliab snapped. "Right now, Father can use you around here. He's not as young as he used to be, you know, and besides, if you leave, who will watch the sheep?"

David winced at his brother's sharp words. He didn't like being called "boy," and he couldn't help it that he grinned a lot. That's just the way he was. It was hard for him to be any other way, and besides, what was wrong with being happy? As far as David was concerned, it was the only way to be.

And why did Eliab have to bring up the sheep at a time like this? Always it was the sheep. The life of a shepherd was the most thankless of all jobs on the farm. David's father assigned him the task of guarding the sheep for days at a time out on the hills surrounding Bethlehem. There was little time for sleep, the food was always the same, and after a while he even began to smell like the sheep. David wrinkled up his nose in disgust. No one else wanted to guard the sheep, but because he was the youngest, the job always fell to him.

David sighed, but there was no use complaining about it. As his mother always said, "It's the faithfulness in doing small tasks that builds character." The thought of these words didn't comfort David much. Not when his three older brothers were marching off the next morning to a great adventure, and he had to stay behind.

Jesse, David's father, stepped into the glow of the warm firelight. The shadows of its flickering flame danced across Jesse's weather-beaten face. The white beard and wrinkles on his face made him appear old and tired, and David noticed how worried he looked. How could he not be worried with his sons going off to fight yet another battle with the hated Philistines?

Jesse reached for Eliab and hugged him affectionately. David saw his father look long and hard at Eliab, and he knew his father was having a difficult time letting his sons go away this time. David tried to imagine what it would be like to send even one son to fight in a battle. His father was giving up three of his eight sons. A tight knot began to creep into the pit of David's stomach at the thought of it all.

LEFT BEHIND

"Eliab, I want you to be careful," urged Jesse. "Those Philistines are barbarians. Their cities and culture may look sophisticated, and they may have all the latest in weapons of war, but they are brutes just the same. And they stand against everything we believe in. Just remember that." Jesse's eyes looked tired and sad. "Promise me you won't envy them for what they have."

"Don't worry, Father," Eliab replied. "Our king is a great leader, and he will help us win the battle against our enemies."

"Well, that's one of the things I'm concerned about, Son." Jesse sounded worried. "I think you have been putting too much trust in the king. He's not the man he used to be when he was young, you know. It's the Lord you should be turning to for courage and victory, Eliab. Never be afraid to put your trust in the Lord our God. He will fight your battles for you."

David thought that Eliab looked annoyed. He couldn't say for sure, but to David, Eliab even seemed a bit impatient. "Yes, Father," was all Eliab would say.

"Oh, and Eliab, please stop by the upper room before you retire for the night. I have something I want you to take to the king for me."

"Yes, Father." Eliab turned to go to the stables to check his mount. Eliab was an officer in General Abner's service, so he rode a mule according to his rank.

It bothered David that Eliab treated Father like that. Actually he felt angry. It was almost as if Eliab didn't respect their father's opinion anymore.

David swallowed hard and shook his head. It was hard not to be annoyed and angry about a lot of things lately. Like not being able to fight in the army. Instead, he had to stay with the dumb sheep. Would he never grow old enough to fight the evil Philistines?

Well, what did it matter? David turned to go to his sleeping quarters. It was late. There was no use hanging around the courtyard or stables any longer. His mother had enough servants on hand to help with the preparations for his brothers. David thought he'd better get some sleep. Tomorrow he'd be going back into the Judean wilderness by himself to tend the sheep on a range of hills northeast of Bethlehem. It could be dangerous out there, but David wasn't afraid. Right now he was just angry at Eliab, more than anything.

David climbed the stone stairway that led to the rooftop of the house. Now that it was spring and the weather had turned warmer, the nights would be pleasant to sleep out under the stars. David lay down on his mat and stretched his tired muscles. He covered himself with the goat-hair blanket his mother had woven for him and looked up at the night sky.

"What a day!" David sighed. Just that morning, word had arrived that the Philistines were on the march again from the city of Gath. Everyone had been in a panic. Some families had even talked of leaving Bethlehem and moving closer to the king's fortified stronghold at Gibeah. And then late in the afternoon, a runner from Gibeah had arrived, calling for men to enlist in the army. The messenger said that the king hoped to raise a larger army than ever before. Eight thousand new troops were being called from the tribe of Judah alone.

And so Eliab, Abinadab, and Shammah had begun making

preparations to leave in the morning. That's when David had been called in from the fields where he had been tending the sheep. His mother had wanted to make sure that David had a chance to see his brothers before they left.

David turned on his mat and tried to get more comfortable. The more he thought about the Philistines, the more he wanted to hate them. He wanted to hate them for the wars they brought on Israel and for the hundreds of Israelites they had killed. He wanted to hate them for the taxes they charged. He wanted to hate them for being pagan and worshiping gods of wood and stone and gold.

It was easy to hate the Philistines, but David knew he shouldn't. "Hate is not a good thing," his mother often said, "even if it's toward the Philistines. It's like a slow poison eating away at your heart."

David frowned in the darkness. It didn't really matter how he felt or how he should feel. The Philistines were invading his country again, and David just wanted to go and help drive them back. He was sixteen years old. He might not be twenty-one, the age required to be a full-fledged soldier in the service of the king, but he could still fight. He could use a sword or spear just about as well as any soldier.

Of course a shepherd's sling was his favorite weapon. Some people scoffed at the idea of using a sling to fight battles, but it worked for David. While out on the hills surrounding Bethlehem, David had used his sling to fight against wild animals that dared to attack his sheep. And then there were the raiding gangs of bandits who tried to sneak in and steal his sheep.

David yawned. There was no doubt about it. He could fight if necessary, but he knew his mother and father would never allow it, and neither would the officers in the king's army. It was no use wishing. For now, he would just have to be content with hanging around home and caring for the sheep on the hills of Judea.

David closed his eyes. Tomorrow would arrive soon enough. Right now he just wanted to sleep. A soft wind brushed against David's face, bringing peace to the end of a hectic day. "Surely God's presence is here," David whispered to himself. He began to recite the words from a song he often sang while tending his sheep. "I cried out to the Lord, and He answered me from His holy mountain. I lay down and slept, yet I awoke in safety, for the Lord was watching over me."

The leaves on the trees rustled in the darkness, and the evening insects played their little songs in harmony with the words of David's prayer. It was as if all nature wished to sing the boy a lullaby, but David didn't hear them. He was already sound asleep.

THE LAZY SERVANT

The dew was still on the grass when David pulled himself up on a rocky ledge overlooking the Jordan Valley far away to the northeast. He shaded his eyes with his hand to get a better view. The sun was playing hide-and-seek with the shadows as they crept away into the cracks and crevices of the ravines and canyons. Birds flitted here and there, and now and then a coney peeked out of its den to see what the day had to offer.

David frowned and kicked a stone as he scanned the rugged ravines below him. *Where are the sheep?* he wondered. *And where is Shimei?*

Shimei was one of the servants in David's father's household. When David had been called home the day before to say goodbye to his brothers, Shimei had been sent out to watch the sheep for David. At least, that had been the plan.

But now the sheep were nowhere in sight. *I knew this would happen!* David squinted in the brightening sun. Shimei was several years older than David and considered himself a man, but as far as David was concerned, Shimei was lazy and irresponsible.

Everyone knew that a shepherd had to be vigilant and watchful, ready to protect the sheep with his life, and David knew that Shimei was not that kind of man.

He's more like a child! David shook his fist at the sky. *Just wait 'til I catch him!* David had tried to tell his father that the sheep were not safe with Shimei, but his father had insisted that "everyone deserves a chance to prove himself."

The sheep weren't at the cave where David usually kept them. He had already checked there. David could hardly imagine that Shimei had taken the sheep much farther north.

He shifted his eyes east toward the sun now racing toward open sky. "I hope he hasn't taken the sheep down toward the Salt Sea," David groaned out loud. "I've told him not to do that! Roving bandits from Moab sometimes crossed the Jordan to raid the countryside on the West Bank. They would love to have a sheep or two to roast over their evening campfires."

The thought of such a thing made David angry. He had never liked Shimei that much, and this wasn't helping any. David carefully picked his way down the side of a rock-strewn hill and then hopped from a rocky ledge.

"Whoa! What's this!" David shouted as he nearly tripped over the sleeping form of Shimei! "Hey! Shimei! What are you doing sleeping here at this time of the morning! Where are the sheep?" David glanced around quickly, but couldn't see them anywhere. Nearby was a small cave. He walked to the mouth of the tiny cave—it was obvious that the sheep had spent the night there, but it was empty now.

David walked back to where Shimei was laying on the ground. He wanted to kick at Shimei's sleeping form, but he tried to control his anger. "Shimei!" he growled. "Get up! The sheep are gone! If I had any sense, I'd thrash you right here and now!"

Shimei turned onto his side, but didn't open his eyes. Suddenly David's nose caught the scent of wine. Lying to one side of Shimei's bedroll was an empty wineskin. David was furious! Anyone who had any sense knew that drinking and herding sheep in the hills of Judea just didn't mix. It was too dangerous for both the sheep and the shepherd. There were wild animals—sometimes roving bandits—prowling about. David gritted his teeth. *Shimei is crazy! How can he drink and keep a clear head to deal with all these dangers?*

As far as important jobs go, being a shepherd was just about at the bottom of the heap. Most people hated the idea of being a shepherd. Sheep were smelly and stupid and totally unpredictable. But to forsake them? Never. David would rather spend endless days and cold nights caring for the sheep than to risk the life of even one sheep.

"Get–up–Shimei!" David spoke the words slowly and deliberately to show he meant business. "Get your things and go home where you belong! You aren't a true shepherd! How could you let the sheep run like this! You couldn't possibly know if the sheep were in danger!" David scowled. "A shepherd is willing to stay with his sheep and protect them with his life."

Shimei stretched, scratched his head and scruffy whiskers, and then slowly got to his feet.

David glared at Shimei and kicked at the empty wineskin. "Now which way are the sheep?"

Shimei squinted his bleary eyes. He pointed in the direction of a small gully. "The sheep were down there the last time I checked. They wanted to eat, so I let them out."

"Let them out!" David raised his hands in exasperation. "Of course you should let them out, but not if you're going to go back to sleep! Shimei! I can't believe this! I've told you before that you never let the sheep out of the fold or the cave unless you are going to watch them! All kinds of predators would love nothing more than to have a lamb for breakfast, or a whole sheep for that matter."

David stalked off. He knew that if he stayed and talked to Shimei much longer, he might become violent.

Fortunately for the sheep, and for David, it wasn't long before he found them. They were just over a ridge to the west, and he lost no time in rounding them up, taking time to count them twice.

When he was sure they were all with him, he checked them for cuts and bruises. One of them was limping badly. It was Jochebed. David had names for all the sheep—there were Aggi, Jezebel, Sheba, and of course the ram, Ezra.

Not far from the cave where the sheep had bedded down for the night, David found a spring seeping out of a rock. At the base of the rock, the water formed a shallow pool, and it was here that David took his sheep for a long drink. Evidently Shimei had not bothered to water them since David had gone home the day before, because the sheep stayed at the spring longer than usual.

As the sun marched past noon, David led the way up a small hill to a cliff that provided shade. The sheep needed rest, and from this lookout, they'd be safer from predators. However, he checked the area for snakes and scorpions. There was nothing like a hot day to bring the most deadly creatures together in one place. David also tested the wind to see that he and the sheep were downwind from the cliffs above him. He wanted to be sure that predators lurking in the rocks above him would not smell the sheep and come looking for an afternoon meal. It was always better to be safe than sorry.

Even so, David was sure that they were probably being watched. Come nightfall, he would have to be especially careful. David always made it his business to avoid the large groves of trees down toward the Jordan Valley. When there were large trees or bushes, a hungry bear was likely to be hiding, and maybe even a lion or two. But to some animals it didn't seem to matter much. Out in the open country, packs of wolves could often be seen walking around in broad daylight.

As afternoon wore on, David found himself wishing that his nephew Joab would come around to keep him company. Joab was the son of David's older sister, but the two boys were more like brothers or best friends.

Together they made quite a pair. David was sixteen years of age, and Joab was fourteen. David had dark hair, almost black, while Joab's was a lighter shade of reddish brown. David was fun-loving and warm-hearted, while Joab tended to be more serious about life. Joab was spiteful sometimes and unforgiving, often holding grudges for months at a time.

They had their differences, but they always had such fun together. Target practice with a shepherd's sling was one of their favorite pastimes. They often got into scuffles about who was more accurate with a bow and arrow, and, of course, they always argued about who was better at charming girls. They told stories around the campfire at night, and they even sang together sometimes. David had a marvelous voice, deep and resonant even at this early age. He was also very good at playing a lyre, an ancient stringed instrument he had bought from the Ishmaelite traders. Joab couldn't carry a tune in a bucket.

Unfortunately, Joab wasn't there, and David was growing drowsier by the minute. If he was going to get any sleep, he knew he needed to catch a few winks while the sheep were safely bedded down in the shade. Who knew what the night shadows would bring. David wanted to be alert to any and all dangers that might arise when the sun was set.

The minty smell of hyssop filled the air, and David could hear bees buzzing from flower to flower. Somewhere far away over the hills, turtledoves were calling out their mournful songs. It was springtime. Could there be a more peaceful feeling than to be out here under the great open sky?

At some point David must have drifted off, but suddenly he was wide awake. He couldn't tell how long he had been sleeping or what had awakened him, but all was not well.

Was it a certain sound he had heard? Was it a change in the direction of the wind? Was it the pungent odor of a lion that passed his nostrils in the afternoon air? His ears listened for the slightest sound that might be out of the ordinary. His sharp eyes scanned the Kidron Valley stretched out beneath him. And then somewhere down below to his right, maybe one hundred paces away, he caught sight of a movement among the rocks.

It was almost imperceptible, but it was there. Only the eye of a trained shepherd would have seen the movement, and David knew that it probably spelled danger.

He shaded his eyes from the glaring sun that was now slanting in from the west and slowly stood to his feet to get a better view. Strange prickles ran down David's spine. He felt a sudden urge to run down to the rocks below and flush whatever it was out of hiding, so that he could face it squarely. But he resisted. As any good shepherd should know, this could be a trick by a predator or an enemy. It could be a wild beast or a gang of roving bandits trying to sneak in and steal away a lamb or sheep.

Whatever it was, David remained rooted to the spot. He would stand his ground. If anyone was going to make a move, it would have to be the hunter.

UNDER ATTACK

Somewhere above him on the cliff, David heard a stone rattle. It wasn't a large stone, but it was there just the same, and to David it signaled trouble. What happened next happened so fast, that in the days following the incident, David never did quite put the whole thing together. All he really remembered later was crying out, "Lord, help me!"

In the next instant, he caught sight of a tawny shape leaping from the outcropping of rock not fifteen paces away. The beast hurtled through the air and landed in the middle of the flock of sheep, knocking several of the ewes and lambs to the ground. The rest of the flock scattered in every direction. In a flash the beast grabbed a helpless lamb off the ground and turned to make its escape.

It was a large female lion, and David knew that to tangle with her could mean certain death for him. If he had had time, David might have argued with himself that the lamb was probably already dead, and it was, after all, only a lamb. Better that David live another day to protect the whole flock, than to risk getting hurt and maybe even death to rescue the poor lamb.

But those would have been only passing thoughts. In an instant, David knew he had no real choice. His instincts told him what he had always known as a shepherd—that the weakest of the flock needed him most.

David sprang into action. His hand was already in his shepherd's pouch searching for a smooth, round stone. Quickly he slipped the stone into his sling and then whirled it around his head. The stone flew straight in the direction of the escaping lion. The lion didn't have a chance, because the stone caught her squarely and brought her down.

With a burst of speed David raced forward and landed on top of the stunned lion. At that same moment, he snatched his knife from its sheath and grabbed the lion's beard. David twisted the lion's head sideways and upward, and with one quick motion of the knife, the lion was dead.

The fight was over almost as soon as it had started. David pried open the lion's jaws and tenderly freed the lamb's body. Miraculously, the lamb was not injured. That fragile little creature had been in the beast's fangs, but it had no broken bones and no lacerations. David set the little lamb on its feet. He was still trying to catch his breath, when he heard a shout. Turning, he saw a boy coming up over the ridge of hills to the south. It was Joab, David's best friend.

"Hey! David, you'll never guess what just happened. I was coming up through the Kidron Valley just now, when I saw this lion sneaking up through those rocks over there." Joab pointed at a cluster of rocks near the far end of the small valley. "Anyway, I grabbed a stone out of my shepherd's pouch and sent it after him. I hit him in the leg, but he got away. He was limping, so he probably won't bother you again for a while."

Joab took a long drink from his water skin. "Good news, David! The spring wheat harvest is in, and the olives are almost ready to pick." Joab jabbered on and on. It was as if he had all but forgotten about the lion he had scared off just moments before.

"Anyway," he continued, "for quite a while now I've been begging my father to let me come up and spend some time with you, so I thought I'd drop in." Joab glanced at David, and then jumped up on a large rock. "What's the matter with you, shepherd boy? You look as if you've seen a—?" Joab stopped short, his mouth hanging open as he suddenly caught sight of the dead lion on the ground in front of David. "Oh—another lion. You killed it?" Joab jumped from the rock and slowly circled the dead body.

"Yeah, I killed it," David wiped the sweat from his forehead with the back of his hand.

"Are you all right?"

"Yeah, I'm OK." David nodded his head slowly and grinned. "How'd you find me?"

"Lucky, I guess. I know you like this area. I just thought I'd give it a shot before I pulled out my ram's horn to signal you." Joab continued staring at the dead lion. "Are the sheep all right?"

David suddenly jumped up. "Whoa! I guess we'd better round them up! The lion gave me quite a scare, and I think I kind of lost track of time for a moment there. Hope we can find them all." David pointed down into the Kidron Valley. "You head off down that way where you saw the other lion, and I'll search up here near the cliffs."

"All right," Joab called over his shoulder, "but how many are we looking for? Do you still have forty-three ewes, or are there more this spring?"

"Forty-seven, and a ram."

"And lambs?"

"Yeah, lambs. There are thirty-two of them."

Within a few minutes, most of the sheep were rounded up. Some of the sheep had quieted down and were already grazing as if nothing had happened. Others where hiding among the rocks and caves along the cliff where David and the sheep had been resting.

Then, while Joab stayed behind to guard the sheep, David searched for the few still missing. The lambs had been easy enough to round up. He finally found the two remaining ewes bleating pitifully near an old watchtower that overlooked the Jordan Valley.

The sun was almost setting on the horizon when David finally arrived back in camp. He found Joab standing over the body of the dead lion. "Whew!" Joab whistled. "Good thing only one of the lions attacked. He must have been an old one, though. Look at his teeth. Some of them are broken."

"Her teeth."

"Huh?"

"Her teeth. He's a she."

"Oh, yeah—I knew that." Joab grinned and then quickly added, "I was wondering, why would an older lion like this come out in broad daylight to catch a lamb? She should know better. Isn't that taking quite a chance? Wouldn't it be much easier for her to just come by and get a midnight snack?"

"I don't know. Maybe she felt her chances at catching a lamb were better out here in the open. Scattering the flock tends to send most shepherds into a panic, you know. And getting past us into the cave at night would be pretty hard, anyway. She does look older, though. It might be that she just couldn't compete with the younger lions down in the Jordan Valley anymore."

"And maybe she's just not so smart."

"Yeah, maybe." David nodded his head. "Anyway, we'd better get her skinned. We don't want to wait until tomorrow, or the skin will be ruined. Animal skins cure a lot better if we take them off and clean them right away."

The two boys worked a few minutes in silence, beginning with a slit under the lion's chin, then continuing all the way down to the end of the belly.

Joab paused for a moment and stared admiringly at David. "You're a good hunter, David."

David glanced up at Joab's boyish grin. "Oh, well, I don't know about that."

"Well, you are, David, and you know it." Joab chuckled to himself. "I'd like to see what you could do if you had to fight one of those Philistines. If you can take down one of these lions, a Philistine ought to be easy for you."

David shook his head and laughed. "Come on, help me pull this skin on up over the lion's head." The two boys grunted and strained at the tough hide until they worked it loose from the carcass.

David then laid the hide out on the ground and began to scrape it with his knife. "I've been thinking, Joab. With those lions on the prowl, you'd think I would have been scared to death. It's strange, but whenever I get in trouble and call on the name of the Lord, a calm always comes over me, and suddenly I know the Lord is with me. I can feel His presence with me, and I just totally lose all fear."

David stopped scraping the hide to rest his arms. "I couldn't face a lion or a bear without God," he added. "It was God's strength that helped me do it. He knows we need these sheep, and that we can't afford to lose even one. So, when I'm in a fix like I was today, He gives me courage and strength—sometimes even before I ask Him."

"Really?" Joab straightened up. "You're lucky. You make it sound so easy. I wish God would help me like that."

David laid his hand on Joab's shoulder. "He will. It takes faith, Joab, that's all. Just plain faith. There's no other way to explain it. You ask God for something and then believe that He will do it for you."

Joab took a deep breath, and shook his head. "Well, then, David, it's your faith in God that makes you such a brave shepherd and warrior. And that's what you are. You may be only sixteen, but you could probably fight anything or anyone and win. Size wouldn't matter."

"Yeah? Well then, if that's so, all the praise should go to the Lord. When He's ready, I'm willing to go."

"Willing to go?" Joab looked at David and grinned. "I guess you are! I've heard you talk scores of times that you wanted to go with your brothers to battle those heathen Philistines."

David smiled a sheepish grin. "Yeah, I guess I have, but I don't think we should enjoy violence, and we definitely shouldn't be cruel. We're God's people, so it's just not right for us to be that way."

"You're talking crazy again." Joab squinted at David. "If it's the Philistines we're talking about, they all deserve to die."

"Do they?" David's voice sounded far away as he tied leather cords to the corners of the lion skin, and then stretched the skin tight between some wooden pegs he had driven into the ground. He stood up, and then suddenly noticed how dark it had gotten.

"The sun's gone!" David shouted. "We're just standing around talking about whatever, and meanwhile it's getting dark." David slapped Joab on the back. "We'd better get these sheep rounded up and over to the cave under the cliff."

Later that evening, around a warm campfire, the boys ate some of the barley bread and dried figs David's mother had put in his pack. As the dancing flames of the fire flickered on the cave walls, the two boys sat and talked about the future of their people. They talked about the war with the Philistines, about King Saul's leadership, and about God's goodness.

David picked up his lyre and began to tighten and tune the strings stretched over its wooden frame. "You know, Joab, when I think of God's goodness, I'm so grateful to Him. He's given us protection while we're out here with the sheep. He's given me a good friend like you, and He's promised us that one day He will send a Savior to take away our sins. Can we ask for more?"

"And a Promised Land that will soon be free of those nasty Philistines," chimed in Joab.

"That too," added David. He strummed a few chords on the lyre and then began to chant, "Sing a new song to the Lord! Let the whole earth sing to the Lord! Sing to the Lord; praise His name! Each day proclaims the good news that He saves. Great is the Lord. He is most worthy of praise!"

BEST OF FRIENDS

"That's three out of four hits. But can you hit the bull's eye?" David looked at Joab skeptically. "How about that small cave up there on the side of the cliff? Can you get it in there?"

Joab glanced over at David and nodded his head. He reached into his shepherd's pouch and pulled out a small stone the shape of an egg. He swung the sling in a circular motion, faster and faster, until it was a blur. Suddenly he released one leather cord of the sling and let the stone fly. The stone zinged straight to the little cave in the side of the cliff and disappeared inside its murky darkness.

"Whew!" whistled David. "That's pretty good. But can you do this?" Now it was David's turn to show off. He reached into his pouch and pulled out a round, smooth stone. Placing it in the sling, he grasped the sling in his left hand and began swinging it around.

"Same cave." David pointed at the cave in the side of the cliff, and then winked at Joab. *Zing!* The stone went straight to its mark and into its hole.

Joab's mouth dropped open in surprise. "Wow! Where did you learn how to do that?"

"Oh, it's something I've been working on while I spend these endless days out here in the wilderness."

"Yeah, I can see that you'd get plenty bored out here with nothing much to do, but why use your left hand?" Joab was puzzled. "It seems that you could be so much more accurate with your right hand."

David raised his eyebrows. "I hit the mark, didn't I? Now, Joab, let's say you're in a battle someday, and your right arm is injured. What then?"

"Good point. Very clever," Joab grinned in admiration. "Do you think you could teach me how to do that?"

David grinned. "I think we could manage it."

The boys practiced slinging stones with their left hands all that morning and into the afternoon. Joab was beginning to get the hang of it, when they heard the tones of a ram's horn, and then a voice calling, "Daaaaavid! Daaaaavid!"

David reached for the ram's horn hanging from his belt and blew two long, low tones out across the hills and valleys of the countryside below him. He waited for a few seconds and then blew the horn again.

Within minutes Shimei came panting over the brow of a high hill. "Oh, there you are, David. I've been looking for you for nearly two hours. Your father has called you home."

"You walked all this way by yourself? What a surprise!" David didn't try to hide his sarcasm. He was still angry with Shimei over his treatment of the sheep the day before. David put another stone in his sling. "What does my father want, Shimei? You came at least seven or eight miles—it must really be important."

Shimei tossed his head a bit disdainfully. "I didn't want to come, but there was no one else to do it. I always have to do all the unpleasant tasks." He rolled his eyes.

"So is there anything more you need to tell me, Shimei?"

"Your brothers have come home again. False alarm with the Philistines, I guess. Anyway, I don't really know what this is all about, but the prophet Samuel is asking that you be allowed to come to a feast. Your father said that you needed to stay with the sheep, but the prophet insisted that you come immediately. He has come to Bethlehem to see your father, actually, and to sacrifice." Shimei stopped to catch his breath. "Now, you've got to hurry! They're waiting for you at the house right now. I guess I'm supposed to stay with the sheep."

"Joab is here," David retorted without even looking at Shimei.

David turned to Joab. "Would you be willing to stay with the sheep until I get back? I'm sure I won't be that long. Tomorrow morning, at the latest."

"Yeah, I can stay that long. You go on and see what's up, but hurry back. I want to work on being a lefty some more. Maybe by the time you get back, I'll be as good as you."

David grinned at Joab. "Not likely, my friend, but you can always dream."

An hour later David was jogging down the lane that led to his house. He stopped to smooth down his hair and pick the burrs and strands of grass from his clothes.

Zerah, chief servant of Jesse's household, met David at the gate to the courtyard and took him out back to the servants' quarters. He made David wash himself in a washbasin and then get into a fresh change of clothes. "Whew! That's more like it." Zerah held his nose. "You shepherds are the worst! You never take a bath, and you smell worse than the stables."

David grinned over his shoulder as he went into the courtyard. "Thanks, Zerah. You're the best—you're always making me look good."

"Well, I don't do it for you, young man. I do it for your father." Zerah slapped David good-naturedly on the shoulder. He liked David. Everyone liked the boy. What was there not to like? The young man was pleasant and polite. He was kind and thoughtful to all the servants and the women in the household. And he was good-looking in a rugged, outdoors sort of way. To Zerah that was the most surprising thing of all. David was handsome, yet it hadn't occurred to him that he was. It hadn't ruined him as it often did other young people who came from important families.

When David entered the courtyard, he saw that his brothers were milling about, talking among themselves. They were all dressed in their best. In spite of David's bath and change of clothes, he felt conspicuous.

Why had he been asked to come home? He didn't feel comfortable at these kinds of get-togethers. Everyone always had to put on such airs and act so stuffy and polite.

And why has the prophet come to offer a sacrifice to the Lord? David wondered. *Why is everyone having this feast in the middle of the week, on a day that isn't a holiday or regular feast day? Why? Why? Why?* David's mind was full of questions—and then suddenly, from across the courtyard, the aged prophet Samuel was looking at him.

A Secret Meeting

"David! I'm glad you came so quickly." The sun was just setting as Jesse took David's arm and pushed him toward the prophet Samuel.

"This is my youngest son, David. He's been with the sheep." Jesse's sun-bronzed face smiled broadly. "David is quite a shepherd! When he's out there, I never worry about the sheep. I think he must sleep with one eye open."

But the prophet Samuel apparently needed no introduction to the young man standing before him. The prophet's shoulders were stooped with age, and he wore a hooded mantle to cover his balding head, but his eyes shone with a strange light. He stared at David as though this was the greatest moment of his life.

David glanced around the courtyard and noticed that everyone else was looking at him too. He felt embarrassed and began to blush. No one said a word. The place was so quiet that it seemed the world had come to a standstill.

After what seemed like an eternity to David, the prophet finally spoke, looking straight at David, his words full of meaning. "This is the one. This is the one whom the Lord has chosen."

David looked around the courtyard again in surprise. *The one whom the Lord has chosen? What is this all about?* he wanted to ask, but he didn't dare. The moment was too solemn. Every single person in the courtyard was older than he. It wasn't really his place to speak unless he had been spoken to, so he just grinned and said nothing.

The prophet Samuel stroked his white beard and turned to Jesse. He nodded his head in wonder, "This is the one—and to think that we nearly passed him by."

The prophet reached into the folds of his cloak and took out a small ram's horn of oil. He placed his hand on David's shoulder and asked him to kneel. No one said anything as the prophet Samuel poured the horn full of oil on top of David's head. David bowed his head and prayed silently as the oil dripped down through his hair and onto the back of his neck. Jesse searched the prophet's face for an explanation, but Samuel only said, "We can begin the evening meal now. Thank you for going to so much trouble, Jesse. You have always been a good friend to me, and today you have made an old man happy." The two elderly men embraced.

As David got to his feet, Zerah brought the prophet Samuel a cup of grape juice. Lifting the cup in his outstretched hand, the prophet turned to the guests in the courtyard. The prophet laid his hand on David's shoulder again. "Friends, we have already offered our sacrifice of a young heifer to the Lord. He has been good to us, for He has promised us salvation and safety if we will obey Him. Let us rejoice and be grateful now to the Lord our God, who brings strength to the young and health to the aged."

The prophet Samuel turned to Jesse. "May the Lord bring prosperity to your household and your fields," he said. "May your crops be abundant this year and your livestock continue to be fruitful. And may your many sons honor you always." The prophet smiled and reverently lifted his hands to heaven. "And now, my children, may the God of our fathers give us peace, as He has done for His people in ages past. Amen."

A resounding amen echoed all over the courtyard as the prayer ended. Almost immediately a group of musicians struck up a merry tune. There were flutes, tambourines, and harps.

And there was food. Pots of bubbling beans and lentils arrived, along with the flat loaves of crusty brown bread. Finally the main dish was brought out—a huge platter of roast beef.

Everyone began to eat, and what a feast it was! David couldn't remember when they had eaten better or when there had been a more distinguished guest in their home.

Then, too, David couldn't help noticing the girls who had come out to serve the evening meal. There were five or six of them, but the prettiest of them all was Abi, a girl about David's age. Her deep brown eyes smiled at him as she passed by with yet another planter of food.

Before long, someone asked David if he would join the musicians. They brought him his lyre, and soon he was playing with the best of them. Not a slow, put-you-to-sleep tune, but a toe-tapping song that got everyone to their feet. There was hand-clapping and foot-stomping. It was soon obvious that David's playing had become the life of the party.

Later that evening, Zerah tapped David on the shoulder. "The prophet wishes to see you outside," he whispered. "He's out by the stables."

David glanced around and for the first time noticed that the prophet had left, but no one else seemed to have noticed. Everyone was eating and laughing and having a good time.

David got up and went out through the back gate. He found the prophet at the feeding mangers, standing among the mules, running his hand down their sleek necks and talking softly to them. The full moon was shedding its bright light over the old man and the mules.

"Hello, Son. This is a blessed day in Israel." The prophet smiled at David. "I'm glad the servants were able to find you this afternoon. Your arrival at the feast tonight was indeed a breath of fresh air."

David looked at the prophet. *What is going on?* he thought. *Why was I called back home from watching over the sheep in the wilderness? What does the prophet want with me? And why was everyone so silent when I walked into the courtyard a few hours ago?*

"I know you must be wondering what this is all about," the prophet added, almost as if he could read David's thoughts. "Let me explain.

"I came here this afternoon on the Lord's business." The prophet chuckled to himself and smiled. "There's rarely a time when I'm doing anything other than the Lord's business. However, this time it's a bit different." The old man stepped closer to David. "The Lord has asked me to come to Bethlehem, to this house, to find a special young man for a special job. When I arrived, I was introduced to your older brothers one by one. I must admit that when I saw Eliab, I felt sure he was the man for the job. He's so noble looking and tall, and has obvious leadership qualities. I waited for the Lord to give me His nod of approval that this might be the one He has chosen." The prophet shook his head solemnly. "But the Lord was silent.

"And then your brother Abinadab was brought to me, and I felt he must be the one. He is intelligent and handsome, but again the Lord was silent. And the same thing happened with each of your seven brothers. I'm sure your father must have been wondering what was going on. Here I was. I had traveled all the way from Ramah, and I was beginning to look foolish. Why had I even come?" The prophet paused and shook his head. "You can imagine how I must have felt. I knew that God had brought me here for a reason, but what was it?"

The old man smiled. "And then by chance, I happened to ask your father if he had any more sons. I don't know why I asked. I had assumed that when I asked him to have his sons attend, he would bring them all. And then when he said there was one more son—you—but that you were out with the sheep, it hit me like a load of bricks. You were the one! I could feel it in my bones! Before you even arrived, I just knew that you had to be the chosen one in Israel."

The prophet stopped for a moment to let his words sink in. "I knew, then, that my trip here had not been in vain. And when you walked through that courtyard gate and I saw your face, I was even more sure that you were the one. All I could say was, 'Praise God! Here is a young man after God's own heart!' "

David stared at the aged man. *What is the prophet talking about? What is he driving at? What am I missing?* Here David was being ushered into the presence of probably the greatest man in Israel since Joshua, and still he didn't have a clue as to what this was all about.

The prophet Samuel laid his hand on David's shoulder. "And so now you are wondering, What's this all about?"

David nodded his head slowly not knowing what to say. He didn't notice the sounds of the evening that pressed in around him. He didn't hear the mules crunching their grain as they ate or the peepers in the marsh south of the stables. He didn't see the moths fluttering around the burning torch just outside the courtyard gate. All he knew was that something very unusual was taking place at this moment, and he was right in the middle of it.

The prophet looked at David, his eyes piercing the darkness. "God has chosen you for a special task, my son."

David's mouth dropped open in shocked surprise. For several long moments he couldn't speak. *Did I actually hear the prophet say what I think he said?* David wondered. *It doesn't make sense! Why me? I'm just a shepherd boy!*

David took a deep breath and finally opened his mouth. He just had to say something, but a sudden movement in the darkness caught his eye. It was somewhere out past the mangers where the mules and donkeys ate their grain and hay. "Who's there?" demanded David as he stepped toward the mangers, but no one answered.

David peered into the blackness of the night. *Who could it be?* As he stepped toward the feeding mangers, suddenly David's heart began to race. Beads of sweat gathered on his forehead as he thought of who might be lurking in the shadows. Could it be that someone was spying on them? It occurred to David that news about the anointing of a boy by the prophet Samuel would travel very fast in Bethlehem and throughout Judah.

"Who is it, my son?" The prophet sounded concerned as he came to where David was standing.

David continued to search the darkness, but he saw no further movement. Whoever had been there was gone now.

THE NIGHT STALKER

David jumped across a rocky crevice and climbed over a large boulder in his pathway. He stopped to catch his breath as he remembered the events from the day before. *Is it all true? Was I really with Prophet Samuel just last night? Did he really say that I am going to be a leader in Israel?* It all seemed like a dream to David now that he was back in the hills of the Judean wilderness.

He gripped his shepherd's rod tightly in his hand and whacked the ground where a poisonous viper was trying to cross the rocky trail in front of him. Picking up a rock, he threw it at the snake and sent it slithering back under the ledge from where it had come. David shuddered. Poisonous snakes were always a problem in this part of the hill country and dangerous to have around the sheep. One could never be too careful.

David shifted his leather pack from one shoulder to the other. It was a long walk to the range of hills where he had left Joab the day before, but David was used to it. His legs were muscular from running through these hills all day as he chased stray sheep and scared off predators.

Joab was practicing with his sling when David arrived.

"Hey, you're getting pretty good at that." David raised his eyebrows. "I think you've almost mastered that left-handed shot. Want to have a little contest?"

"No thanks, I'd better not stay. I've got to get back home. Father needs me and will wonder where I am if I don't get back soon."

David watched as Joab walked down through the Kidron Valley and disappeared over the top of a hill. He was sorry to see Joab go. It was always more fun when Joab was around. He was a good friend—and a good shepherd too.

The weather was getting hotter now that summer was approaching. It was still easy to find green grass in the hills, and most of the mountain springs would be flowing for several weeks to come. Now and then something unusual would happen to keep David on his toes, but for the most part, the days tended to run together when David was by himself.

Several mornings later while watering the sheep at a mountain spring, David crouched on the ground to examine the tracks of a large animal. "Hey! These are bear tracks!" David exclaimed. He glanced around at the surrounding landscape and then back at the tracks. "Hmmm, I wonder if these are old Ahab's tracks." David tried to follow the tracks as they led away from the spring, but the tracks disappeared among the nearby rocks.

As the sheep gathered around for their daily drink, David turned to Ezra, the large ram that always kept a watchful eye out for the flock. "We never can quite catch him, can we, Ezra?" David grinned at the wise old ram. "That bear thinks he's the smartest thing this side of the Jordan, but one of these days we're going to teach him a lesson, aren't we, old boy?"

Ezra didn't utter a sound. He just looked at David wisely and then pawed the ground.

"That's it, Ezra. You tell 'em." David laughed at Ezra's funny antics. The ram really was wise. He had lived longer than any ram David's father had ever had.

But in spite of David's big talk, he actually was worried about the bear. His father and all the shepherds in the region had been talking about this bear for years. Ever since David could remember, he had been hearing stories about the bear attacking flocks of sheep on both sides of the Jordan. He had killed scores of sheep, and had even killed a shepherd boy once. The bear was a legend, all right, and now it looked as if he was in the area again.

"I'd know that large paw print anywhere." David frowned as he knelt on the ground. "It's got a slash mark across the inside of the left back foot. He must have got it in one of his fights with the local shepherds or something."

At his noonday meal David stopped to rest under an old oak tree. He wondered what he was going to do about old Ahab. With sheep in the area, the bear was most likely going to be a problem. As he planned his strategy against the bear, David pulled a roll of cheese from his shoulder pack and cut off chunks with his knife. He ate a few handfuls of raisins and parched grain and then drank from the water skin he kept hanging in the shade of the tree.

David glanced over at Ezra lying in the shade with the rest of the flock. "Well, Ezra, I guess we're going to just have to get out a few tricks of our own." David laughed in spite of the seriousness of the situation. It helped him be less afraid. He rummaged around in his pack and brought out some bear claws that he had taken from a bear he had killed two years before. David held the claws up and winced. "Pretty ugly lookin' claws, aren't they, Ezra? Bet these would do some damage."

David reached up as high as he could on a tree trunk and swiped the bark with the bunch of bear claws in his hand. He gave Ezra a wink. "I learned that from an old shepherd who used to work for my father." David enjoyed talking to his sheep, but especially old Ezra. It was as if the two of them had something in common—*mostly the good of the sheep,* thought David.

"Now, when old Ahab comes prowling around here to get something to eat, he'll find these claw marks on the trunk of this tree and wonder what bear has been here before him. And since the bear that wore these claws is already dead, old Ahab won't know what to think." David laughed right out loud. "That'll serve him right."

All that afternoon the ram faithfully watched over the flock. He barely even took time to graze with the rest of the sheep. David could tell that the ram was wary of something. Now and then Ezra would lift his nose to the wind as if he were checking for the scent of a bear. As the sun began to sink in the west, David knew he needed to bed the sheep down earlier than usual. He led the sheep up a small ravine to a large cave in the side of a steep cliff, so that the sheep would be protected on three sides.

As a final precaution for the night, David brought out a small piece of lion skin that he had saved in his pack from his fight with the lion a few days back. He wrapped the skin around a rock, tied it up with a leather cord, and then walked all around the edge of his little camp dragging the bundle behind him. "There," sighed David as he returned to camp and began to build a fire. "That'll confuse old Ahab even more. He won't know what to think with the smell of lion everywhere."

David knew he dared not sleep at all. The sheep were safely bedded down for the night inside the cave, and David had sat down between the cave and the fire, but he still felt uneasy. Now and then, during the night, Ezra got up and paced back and forth inside the cave like a sentry. *Does the old ram sense the bear is nearby?* David wondered.

The hours passed, and David's eyelids began to grow heavy. He knew he needed to get up and move around, but a sluggish stupor seemed to come over him, and try as he might, he just couldn't shake it. Finally he nodded off. It was just for a few moments, but it was enough.

In that instant the bear made his move. In his hiding place among the rocks, the old bear had waited until he sensed the boy was growing sleepy. Then when the fire had burned low and it was well past midnight, the beast came charging out of the darkness and straight for the mouth of the cave.

The noise wakened David, and in an instant he took in the whole situation. Coming through the darkness at a full gallop was the shaggy form of a black bear. His head was bobbing up and down, and his teeth were bared to the gums. In the glint of the dim firelight David caught the look in the bear's beady eyes—a look of evil, mischief, and just plain hunger.

David rolled out of the path of the oncoming bear to avoid his sharp slashing claws. He jumped to his feet, but the bear lumbered right past him and into the cave where the sheep were bedded down. David knew that the bear had only one thing on his mind, but he couldn't believe the bear was being so reckless. Had he no fear of man?

Seconds later, the bear emerged from the cave, and David gasped. The bear had a little lamb in his jaws. There was no time for David to be angry with himself for falling asleep. There wasn't time to ask himself why he had allowed the bear to get past him and into the cave. The only thing David could do now was react, as any shepherd should. He would fight for the life of this lamb.

The bear took one look at David and came charging past him, but David was ready for him. He snatched up a log lying beside the fire, and hit the bear with all his might.

Now it was the bear's turn to be angry. With a roar he dropped the lamb, reared up on his hind legs, and turned to face David! In the darkness, the dim silhouette of the bear appeared taller than David. Swinging his paws from side to side, he growled and snarled and then lunged at David!

David was terrified, but he didn't give an inch! He ducked around the bear and behind him, but the brawny bear swung a backhanded paw and knocked David to the ground! David scrambled to get to his feet, but it was too late! The bear was upon him!

"Help me, Lord!" was all David could scream in those brief moments. Without even thinking David snatched his knife from the sheath at his side and rolled over to face the slashing teeth and swinging paws of the bear. As the bear's body came down upon David, the sharp knife found its mark.

With a groan, the bear rolled to one side and fell heavily across David's legs. David pushed the great black hulk off of him and slowly stood to his feet. He shook his head, and for several long minutes he just stared at the dark form of the bear on the ground. It was Ahab, all right.

Trembling, David returned to the fire and threw some more wood on it. "Thank You, Lord," he whispered as he sat down again. "I guess my little tricks to keep Ahab away didn't work." David wiped the sweat from his forehead and then went to check on the sheep. He held a lighted torch high over his head inside the dimly lit cave. The sheep seemed to be all right. Even the little lamb had revived and was back with its mother. Fortunately for David, the bear had been alone, and this had saved both him and his flock.

Later in the wee hours of the morning, as David sat by the blazing fire now heaped high with wood, he wondered what other dangers lurked in the darkness. He really felt on edge now as he watched the fire make ghostly patterns dance on the rocks and the cave walls behind him.

This is foolish, thought David. *I need to calm down. God is here, and He has delivered me from Old Ahab.* David took a deep breath and reached for his lyre. He strummed the strings of the instrument and began to sing the words to a song that had been running through his mind for several days. "Do not be afraid of the terrors of the night, nor the arrow that flies in the day. If you make the Lord your refuge, no evil will conquer you. For He will order His angels to protect you wherever you go."

As the first pink streaks of dawn pushed their fingers over the edge of the horizon to the east, David smiled to himself. As always, God was the one sure thing in life that he could count on. It made David feel safe just to think about it.

A MYSTERY SOLVED

The morning was clear, and the birds had been up for hours. David stretched his arms high over his head and yawned as he watched the lambs skipping about, their tails wiggling.

How was a shepherd ever to get any sleep on the job? With no one else around to help, David couldn't afford to catch a nap during the morning hours because the sheep moved about too much while grazing. During the afternoon hours the sheep usually rested for an hour or two, depending on the weather. Unfortunately, that was the only time David could really rest, and he wasn't sure he really could do that with all the attacks on the flock lately.

David's thoughts turned toward home as he rummaged in his shoulder pack for something to eat. He bit off a piece of dried fig and savored the sweet taste in his mouth. His food supply was getting pretty low. There were only a few handfuls of parched grain in the pack and some figs. His supply of barley loaves and cheese had long since run out. He would either have to set a snare to catch a wild bird, perhaps a quail, or else hope that another shepherd in the area would have some food to spare. David couldn't afford to leave the sheep even to go home to get more food, but maybe his mother would send out one of the servants to bring some fresh bread and fruit.

David sat down on a rock and picked up his lyre. Maybe if he sang a few songs, he could ignore his growling stomach. He hadn't played more than three or four lines of a song he was composing when the faint tones of a ram's horn sounded from down in the Kidron Valley.

David put his lyre down and stood to his feet. *Was that two long blasts, or three?* He took his own horn from his belt and gave two long blasts. He paused to listen. There it was again—two long blasts. It must be a messenger from home. David blew two more blasts and then sat down with his lyre to wait for the messenger to arrive. It wasn't long before a servant appeared, all out of breath.

It was Mahlon. David liked Mahlon. Next to Zerah, Mahlon was his favorite of all the servants in his father's household. He was short, a middle-aged man, and his mustache and whiskers wiggled comically when he talked.

"You do pick the most remote spots to take your sheep, don't you?" Mahlon took a drink from a water skin slung over his shoulder. "Aren't you afraid to be out here by yourself, David?"

David smiled, "No, not much, I guess. The grass is thicker here because not many shepherds bring their sheep this far into the hills." He stood to his feet, "And besides, the Lord is with me." David pointed to the bearskin now stretched between wooden stakes pounded into the ground.

Mahlon took his shoulder pack off and laid it on the ground. "Whew!" he whistled. "He's big, isn't he?"

"That he is," David chuckled. "It's Old Ahab."

"Old Ahab!" Mahlon knelt on the ground by the bear and whistled again. "You've got nerve, young man! You must be the best shepherd in these parts! Wait until your father and brothers hear about this!" He stood to his feet and laid his hand on David's shoulder. "Do you know how many years shepherds and farmers have been trying to catch this bear?"

David shook his head and laughed a deep throaty laugh. "Well, thanks, Mahlon, but it's the Lord's doing. You can tell my father if you like, but I don't think my brothers want to hear about my adventures out here. I don't know why, but it seems that they're always annoyed with me when I come home."

"Jealous is more like it, I'd say."

David frowned and then shook his head. "You think so?"

"I'm certain of it."

"But why jealous of me? Who wants to be a shepherd?"

Mahlon smiled and his whiskers twitched. "I don't think it has anything to do with your being a shepherd."

"Then what is it they're jealous of?" David searched Mahlon's face for an answer, but Mahlon only smiled. *What is Mahlon thinking?* David could not know that Mahlon was thinking it was because David was handsome and talented with bright intelligent eyes—that every girl in the village talked of him when they gathered at the village well in the evening. David wouldn't have believed it even if Mahlon had told him it was so. He was too shy.

"Your father calls you home," Mahlon changed the subject. "He has a message for you from the royal court, and you are to go home at once."

"The royal court!" David said excitedly. "Do you know what the message is?"

"Not really. You are being asked to play for the king, I think. That's all I know."

David looked at Mahlon as though expecting more, but Mahlon only slapped him on the back. "Go, my son! Don't forget to take your lyre, and may God go with you."

David left the sheep in Mahlon's care. He was glad that Shimei hadn't been sent instead. Even though David had been called home to serve the king, he knew he would never leave the sheep with Shimei again.

David arrived home in the early afternoon. When the servants saw him coming down the footpath to the house, David's father appeared in the doorway to the stables.

"I'm glad Mahlon found you, David. You need to leave immediately so that you can arrive by nightfall. You'll need a donkey so that you can take a gift to the king. I'm sending some of your mother's wheat bread and a skin of our best wine. The donkey is behind the house by the winepress. Huldah will make sure you have everything you need."

Jesse gave David a gentle push in the direction of the donkey. "Oh, and I'm also sending a young goat with you. I've heard it's the king's favorite meat." Jesse smiled at his youngest son. "I'm proud of you, David. Now go, my son, and may the God of our fathers bless your every step."

Behind the house one of the women servants was putting an armload of bread into baskets tied on either side of the donkey.

"Hello, Tirzah. Let me help you with that." David took the leather cords from Tirzah and began to tie the lid on one of the baskets. "You should be resting, Tirzah. How soon are you expecting your baby?"

Tirzah smiled at David. "In another month, I'd say." She patted David on the head. "You're such a good boy, David, always looking out for others."

As she turned and left to go back inside the house, David tied his bedroll and lyre on top of the load.

"Here are two water skins for your trip." David turned at the sound of a girl's voice behind him. It was Abi.

"What are you doing here?" David asked in surprise. He looked past Abi at Huldah standing in the open doorway. She gave David a wink and then disappeared inside again.

David blushed. Someone must have told Abi that he was back from herding sheep in the hills. He smiled to himself. It seemed these women were always trying to play matchmaker.

Abi looked at the ground shyly. "I heard about the request from the king's advisors that you go to the royal court to play for the king, so I came to see you off."

"To see me off? Well, thanks," was all David could say. He turned quickly to tighten the load on the donkey so that she wouldn't see him blush again. He had never been any good with girls. Maybe it was because he never knew what to say.

Abi glanced toward the house and then the stables. "But that's not the only reason I came."

David wondered, *What will she say next?* One could never be sure what a girl would say next. "Actually, David," she glanced around nervously again, "I came to remind you to be careful."

"Careful?" David smiled. "I'll be careful. Don't worry, Abi. I'll take my shepherd's sling and knife, and I'll take only the main roads."

"No, David," Abi insisted. "I'm talking about while you're at the royal court. I'm afraid for your safety there."

David stared at Abi suspiciously. What was she talking about? Why would she be worried about him being at the king's court? David thought about the ceremony with the prophet Samuel. *Does Abi know something about the secret conversation with the prophet out by the stables? How could she?*

"Why would I be in danger at the king's court?" David stammered. "He's my king, and they've asked me to come and play for him."

Abi glanced toward the house and the stables again and then whispered, "I saw the whole thing, David."

"You saw the whole what?"

"I saw you and the prophet the night of the sacrificial feast. You were out by the stables together. I heard the whole thing."

David's mouth dropped open. He didn't know what he should say—or do, but he finally found his voice. "You were sneaking around spying on us?"

"No! No! I wasn't!" Abi sputtered. "I mean, yes, I was, but I wasn't spying. I mean," she took a deep breath, "I mean, I didn't mean to spy."

Abi's face was flushed, and David thought that maybe she would cry.

"Please, David, I didn't mean to spy. I know I shouldn't have been out there at the stables, but I saw you going out to the stables and I wanted to talk to you. Honestly, I didn't know the prophet was there until it was too late. So, I hid behind the mangers, and I heard everything."

David shook his head. "So that was who I heard—and saw!" he added. "I *thought* I saw someone in the shadows!"

Abi looked at the ground. "Please forgive me, David. I know I shouldn't have been there spying, but it's your safety at the court that worries me now. If the king has heard of the anointing, he might get suspicious."

"Why would he be suspicious? I'm nobody important. I'm just a boy!"

"But you were anointed. Lots of people know that by now. Even me."

"Yes, but you were *spying.*" A slow grin began to spread across David's face.

"Please be serious!" Abi begged.

"Well, what shall I do?" David shrugged his shoulders. "I can't just not go!"

"No, I guess not, but promise me that you'll keep your eyes and ears open."

David smiled at the young girl with big brown eyes. "All right, Abi, but you're going to have to promise me that you'll tell no one about the secret meeting I had with the prophet or that we ever had this conversation here today."

Abi smiled an impish grin. "What conversation?"

David tilted his head sideways. "Now look who's not being serious."

"I promise! I promise!" Abi giggled. "But, let's pray right now that God will watch over you while you are at the court."

No one heard Abi and David as they asked God for David's safe return—no one except two sparrows in the grape arbor and a little lizard sunning himself on the stone wall of the winepress.

THE CRAZY KING

David paused at the gate to the king's fortress in Gibeah. The sky had become overcast. Clouds hung low, giving the fortress a bleak appearance.

"Who goes there?" The guard shouted from atop the wall. "State your name and business!"

David swallowed hard. He had known he would be nervous when he finally arrived at the royal court, but he hadn't thought he would be so tongue tied.

"Speak your business!" shouted the guard.

David finally found his voice. "It's—it's me!" He blurted. "David, the son of Jesse of Bethlehem."

The guard did not answer.

"I have come at the royal court's command to provide music for the king," David added.

David heard more shouting inside the fortress wall, and then the large gates made of iron and oak began to creak open. David's first glimpse inside the fortress surprised him. The place looked quite ordinary. He had always hoped that the king's home would be a royal palace with marble walls and well-watered gardens. He had expected to see royal advisers attended by servants dressed in the finest of uniforms, and prancing horses and peacocks strutting around the palace grounds. At least that's what he had always imagined a royal palace should look like.

Instead, he saw an open stone courtyard surrounded by

chambers with long rows of overhanging balconies. Most of the servants hurried about the place in common plain-looking clothes. There were no strutting peacocks and no horses with fine jingling harnesses. David hoped the disappointment didn't show on his face.

"Are you the son of Jesse?"

David turned toward a man who had come from a side door in one of the chambers bordering the courtyard. "Uhh, yes. David, son of Jesse."

"Then you'd better come with me. We're going to have to get you into something presentable."

David scanned the balconies above the open courtyard for a familiar face. He knew of at least one person who worked at the court—his brother Eliab. Eliab wouldn't be here because he had recently returned home from the royal court, but David didn't see anyone else he knew, either.

"I said, you'd better come with me!" The man sounded impatient. "I know you common folk are dumb, but I didn't know you were deaf too."

David was shocked at the man's rudeness. He figured the man had to be one of the king's courtiers, but he didn't like being insulted by anyone, even a royal courtier. David knew his own family wasn't royalty, but they did have servants and a prosperous farm. His father Jesse was an important man in the village too. The town of Bethlehem was small, but as one of the village elders, Jesse helped to make important decisions for the town. Sometimes Jesse even provided lodging for important officials who came through town on the king's business.

"Peasants!" grumbled the courtier more to himself than to anyone in particular. "It's a wonder we can manage to get any decent help at all here at the court!"

David followed the man into one of the chambers along the courtyard and waited for him to rummage through a wooden chest in a corner of the room. The little bit of light that trickled in through a small window opening high on the wall barely lit the darkened chamber.

"Here! Put these on and then report to the audience chamber at the end of the courtyard." The man shoved the clothes into David's stomach, and then added, "Stay outside the door and wait until someone arrives to escort you in." The man turned and disappeared before David could ask any questions.

Later when David reached the large double doors of the audience chamber, he wondered what he would find inside. The courtyard was drab, but certainly the inside chambers of the palace would be more impressive. Certainly they would be more fitting for a king!

"Please step this way," announced a man dressed in a red tunic with an embroidered belt around his waist.

As the two of them entered the large chamber, David's eyes had to adjust to the dimness of the place. It was not at all what he had expected to find at the palace of a king, if one could call this a palace. There were no colorful plants or beautiful tapestries. Sooty torches did their best to light the room, but there weren't enough of them, and the music being played was depressing—or so David thought.

At the far end of the audience chamber, the king sat on a raised platform in the shadows. His elbow was resting on the armrest of his throne, and he appeared to be deep in thought. Beside him on a stand was a clay bowl filled with lighted incense, its smoke spiraling upward. An armed guard in full uniform stood on the other side of the throne, his spear and shield held firmly in his hands. Now and then the light from the flickering torches reflected off the guard's polished helmet.

The courtier in red escorted David to a cushion on the floor among the other musicians. Two musicians were playing flutes, a woman had a tambourine, and another man had a lyre very much like David's. But the flutes sounded mournful, and the woman was tapping out a dull hypnotic rhythm on her tambourine.

David shook his head. The music was awful, and he guessed that it was doing the king more harm than good. If the music was going to be of any help, David knew the royal musicians would have to change their style of music. Something had to be done, but David wasn't sure if he was the one to do it. He couldn't just step in and take over. Not on his first day, at least.

As he settled himself among the cushions, David remembered Abi's advice, *"Be careful! Keep your eyes and ears open."* David chuckled to himself. That should be easy enough from where he sat in the shadows.

Suddenly the king stirred on his throne. "Bring me more wine," he muttered. A courtier standing in the shadows behind the throne clapped his hands. Within seconds a young servant girl came gliding out with a golden goblet on a silver platter. What happened next happened so fast that David wouldn't have believed it, if he hadn't seen it with his own eyes.

Just as she reached the throne, the servant girl tripped on one of the crimson carpets spread out before the throne. The goblet of wine clattered to the floor, spilling the wine on the steps to the throne. In horror the girl let out a gasp and clutched her hand to her mouth, not even daring to raise her eyes to the king. Instantly the king flew into a rage, a flood of oaths pouring from his mouth. The servant girl seemed glued to the spot, but when the king reached for his javelin, she fled toward a side door.

"How dare you be so clumsy!" roared the king. He jumped to his feet and threw the javelin at the girl with all his might. Fortunately, it missed her, but the javelin pinned her flowing tunic to the wooden door frame. The servant girl began to scream hysterically. She fell to the floor yanking and clawing at the tunic, until she finally managed to pull herself free.

No one said a word as the girl ran off shrieking. Soldiers, servants, courtiers, and musicians stared at the king, wondering who would be the next target for the king's anger.

"What are you all looking at!" growled the king. He turned and sat down heavily on his throne.

For a few moments the audience chamber was as silent as a tomb, and suddenly David realized that this was his opportunity to bring a change to the mood of the throne room. Softly he began stroking the strings of his lyre. The rich chords of a beautiful melody began to take shape as David played. Amazingly enough, none of the other musicians joined in. It was as if they were enchanted by the melody, or maybe just afraid to spoil the magic of the moment. As he played, David began singing the words of a song he had sung many times while sitting by the fire, guarding his sheep at night.

"As the deer longs for streams of water, so I long for You, O God. Taste and see that the Lord is good." As the song continued, the chords of David's lyre blended perfectly with the pure tones of his smooth, sweet voice. "The laws of the Lord are true—each one is fair. They are sweeter than honey, even honey dripping from the comb."

When David finally stopped playing some time later, he looked around and realized that the room was nearly empty. The musicians were gone—the servants were gone. Only the guard remained at his post by the throne, and a courtier sat dozing in a chair in the shadows.

"Thank you, my son." David turned in surprise at the sound of the king's deep voice. He had thought that the king must have dozed off.

"You have no idea how soothing your music has been today." The king's voice sounded sad, and David wondered why. "You are very talented," the king added. "Come here and sit down beside me."

David rose to his feet and approached the throne. The king had dark circles around his eyes, but a look of peace had come over him. He looked different from when David had first arrived. David knelt before the king and bowed his head respectfully to the floor.

"I have often wondered if there could be music somewhere that was as beautiful as you have played this afternoon. Today I have been truly blessed. I want to thank you from the bottom of my heart." The king gave David a weak smile and then sighed a long, tired sigh.

"As you can see, I am a lonely man." The king shook his head sadly. "I have ignored God's commands, and for too long now I have done what I wanted to do as king."

The stillness of the throne room pressed in around David, and he wondered if the royal courtroom was always like this.

"What is your name, my son?" the king asked kindly.

David raised himself up from the floor, but he dared not look the king in the eye. It was forbidden for a commoner like David to do so. "My name is David. I'm from Bethlehem." David was so nervous, he forgot to say anything else.

"You are gifted, my son." The king's eyes got a faraway look in them. "With abilities like this, you will be a great man one day, I am sure."

David's heart skipped a beat as he watched the flames of the flickering torches cast their eerie shadows on the king's face. *What did the king mean when he said that I will one day be great? Had he heard about the anointing ceremony with the prophet Samuel?* David trembled, but managed to hide his fear.

"Thank you, my lord. I am your humble servant," was all David could say.

PANIC ATTACK

David hurried to the well of Bethlehem just outside the city gate. He knew he needed to get home, but a cool drink of water must come first. He quickly lowered a water skin into the darkness of the well. The long trip from Gibeah had really made him thirsty. David took big gulps of the clear, cold water—there was nothing like Bethlehem water anywhere.

David turned toward home. He had spent several days at the royal court playing for the king, until a messenger arrived all out of breath to warn the king and his advisors that the Philistine army was on the move once again. They were gathering their forces in the Valley of Elah, the messenger had said.

The king's royal advisors had then sent David home. "For the time being, your services will not be needed at the court," they had said. "The country is at war. When we have need of you again, we will call for you." And with that they dismissed David as though he was in the way.

"If the king has need of my services on the battlefield, I will be glad to serve him there," David had added hurriedly.

But the advisors had dismissed him a second time. "You're too young," they replied. "The king needs experienced men whose hearts do not melt when in the heat of battle, men who do not faint at the sight of blood and the sound of the Philistines' battle cries. The king needs men who know how to use weapons of war, not a boy who chases sheep with sticks."

So that was it. No one needed a young boy of sixteen to do a really important job. David could be left out in the wilderness all by himself to guard sheep. He could risk his life fighting off lions and bears, but fighting the Philistines was considered a man's job. The whole idea made David angry. Adults got to do all the really exciting stuff.

As David stepped through the city gate, he knew things were worse than he had imagined they would be. The entire town was in a panic. David knew that many of the men would be going off to fight the Philistines, but why were the women and children running around too?

David walked though the winding streets of Bethlehem until he reached the outskirts of town on the other side. When he arrived at the family gate, he found his own home turned upside down too. Everyone was scurrying about, and no one even noticed him as he stepped through the open doorway of the courtyard. Some were loading food into baskets. Others were piling loads on donkeys and hitching oxen to carts. The women looked frightened, and little children followed their mothers around clutching at their long, flowing garments. David knew this was more than the usual commotion for sending a few men off to war. It looked as if everyone was preparing to flee the town. But where would they go?

No one seemed to have time to stop and tell David what was happening. David finally grabbed Shimei's arm as he rushed by with an armload of blankets. "What's going on?" David demanded.

"Haven't you heard?" Shimei turned in surprise. "The Philistines are coming with a large army. They've got chariots this time, and it's rumored that they have a secret weapon."

"I know they're coming," David retorted, "but King Saul is gathering an army and going out to meet them. At least that's what I was told at the fortress in Gibeah earlier today."

"That may be!" Shimei had to almost shout over the noise of the family courtyard. "But we've been told that the Philistines are headed this way now, and I think they mean business this time. Why don't you help us get things packed, David? We could use the help."

David almost laughed. For once Shimei was working. Maybe it had something to do with the fact that he was afraid.

"I don't get it, Shimei!" David shook his head in disbelief. "Why are we leaving? This is our town! This is our country!"

"David, if the Philistines arrive, you don't want to be here to meet them." Shimei turned to leave.

David again grabbed Shimei's arm. "Wait a minute! I'll admit that we need to get the women and children out of here, but where will we take them?"

"We're not sure yet." Shimei jerked his arm free and frowned. "How should I know? South, maybe? There're talking about Hebron. It's a great fortress, I hear, and it's in friendly territory."

David stopped in the middle of the courtyard. He was in a daze. Could it be possible that he and his family would have to leave their home! In his wildest nightmares, David had never thought that his family would have to leave home for any reason. This was the land of Judah, the heart of Israel's strength! The tribe of Judah was supposed to be brave—Judah's symbol was a lion! To run away from the Philistines seemed cowardly!

"Why should we leave our land given to us by the Lord?" muttered David. "It doesn't belong to those heathen Philistines! They're an evil nation, that's what they are!"

David found his father in the house. "Is it true what I hear, Father? That we are leaving home because of the advancing Philistine army?"

David's father, Jesse, turned his sad gaze to David. "It is true that many are fleeing, my son. Your mother will be going and taking your sisters and the grandchildren with her. I have released any of the servants who wish to go, but Zerah has agreed to stay behind." Jesse paused and then added, "I will not be going. I cannot abandon our home and farm to those godless Philistines. Our God whom we serve will be our shield."

David suddenly realized how much he admired his father. The man was as brave as any soldier in the field. It was his quiet strength that carried him through troubled times. It was his faith in God.

David rose to his full height. "I will stay with you, Father. I'm not afraid either."

"I know you're not, David. I know I can depend on you. That's why I'm sending you back to stay with the sheep. They're safer there with you than they would be here at home. Mahlon is there with them now, waiting for you to take over so he can get his family to safety. You need to hurry."

David's heart sank. It was the sheep again. Always it was the sheep. *Will I ever be a man? Will I ever be given a real man's job?* David turned to leave so that his father wouldn't see the disappointment on his face. His father had enough things to worry about right now.

"Hey, David, are you going, too?" David turned to see Joab's brother, Abishai, trudging out of the stable leading a donkey loaded with supplies.

"Me?" David wanted to laugh. "Are you kidding? My father already has me assigned to sheep-herding duties!"

David noticed how high the donkey was loaded as it walked by. "Hey! What's all this stuff?" he demanded. *"You're* not leaving town too?"

"Not me!" Abishai shook his fist. "I'm not going! I wouldn't miss the arrival of the Philistines for anything! When those evil villains march into town, I'll be waiting in ambush with my sling and javelin!"

And David knew he would. Abishai was only thirteen, but David knew he could handle a sling better than anyone else in Bethlehem. Better even than David himself. He could out-sling, out-wrestle, out-throw anyone his age, and even some older. Abishai was stocky for his age and tough as a mule. David smiled. He knew that if he ever needed to raise an army of his own, he'd want Abishai to be an officer in it.

"So, if you're not leaving, where are you going with all that stuff?" David pointed at the donkey loaded high with baskets and rolled-up bedding.

"My mother and sisters are leaving town, and father has asked Joab and me to help them with the supplies." Abishai grinned. "But I'll be back as quick as I can," he added.

"You do that, but I hope you're not too late to help us whip the Philistines."

David turned and caught sight of Eliab sitting on a bench in the shade of a mulberry tree. A servant was helping him make some last-minute adjustments to his armor. David was proud of Eliab. He looked so handsome dressed in his colorful military tunic, and wearing a leather coat of armor across his chest. It wasn't as impressive as the metal armor the king and his generals wore, but most of the soldiers in the king's army didn't wear any armor at all. Eliab was a captain in the king's army. One hundred soldiers served under his command, so he rode a mule and even had a metal helmet.

David wished he hadn't already talked with his father about guarding the sheep. Then he could have asked Eliab if he could go to the battlefield with him. There were a thousand-and-one things he could do to make his brother's life easier there. He could take care of Eliab's mule, make Eliab's meals, be his armor bearer— but Eliab would probably have said No, anyway.

David grabbed a water skin and walked to where Eliab was sitting. He offered his brother a drink of water.

"Thanks," was all Eliab would say. He didn't even look at David, but continued to fuss with the leather plates on his armor and then reached for his sword. David wondered. Maybe it still wasn't too late to ask Eliab if he could go along with him to the battlefield. It wasn't likely to happen, but David figured it was worth a try.

"How soon will you be leaving, Eliab?"

Eliab ran his whetstone down the full length of his sword several times, and then touched its edge to test its sharpness. "You're not going," he replied. "I've told you that you're too young, and that's final. Maybe someday you'll be able to prove yourself a man, but right now you're just a boy, so get those foolish notions out of your head about fighting the Philistines!" Eliab said nothing more. He just stood to his feet, slipped his sword into its sheath, and walked off toward the stables.

David's mouth dropped open, but he said nothing. What could he say? It was no use trying to be nice. Eliab was so full of himself that he didn't even have time to think of what others might want. David knew he would have done anything to please Eliab, anything to make him happy. He would climb the highest mountain or cross the deepest river, if that's what Eliab wanted. He would fight the fiercest of enemies and stand back-to-back with Eliab in battle. David knew he would be willing to give his life for Eliab, if that's what it took. All David wanted was for his brother to give him a little respect. David knew he was young, but a big heart should count for something, shouldn't it?

And maybe that was the problem. Maybe David wanted all the right things for all the wrong reasons. Maybe respect and acceptance were not things that others could give to you. Maybe you just had to earn them because of who you were and how you lived.

And maybe faith in God had something to do with it. If David did his best in the small tasks of life, maybe God would honor that. If he served his country and his God, and if he waited patiently for God to work in his life, then maybe everything would work out for the best.

David went to get a fresh change of clothes and some food supplies. No use sitting around and getting in the way. He had a job to do, and it couldn't wait. The sheep needed him, and right now that was all that mattered.

A Narrow Escape

David put an egg-shaped stone in his sling. He surveyed the landscape and chose a small cave high up on the side of a cliff. Grasping the long strands of his leather sling, he began to swing it in wide circles above his head. Faster and faster went the smooth stone in the leather pouch at the end of the sling. With a sudden jerk of his wrist, David released the stone, and it sped toward its mark.

He took a deep breath of fresh air. It felt good to be free. Free from being cooped up inside, free to be in the great outdoors again and to be his own boss. No one to tell him what to do, and no one to make him feel like a child. Sure, having to guard the sheep day in and day out was hard at times, but it had its advantages.

Now, being at the royal fortress in Gibeah—that was really something! Playing for King Saul was OK, but David never was quite sure when the king would fly into one of his fits of rage. At any moment he might just start throwing things. Was the king losing his mind? Was he going crazy? No one could say for sure. One rumor even said that a demon possessed the king's soul after he had forsaken God.

The thought of the king being possessed by an evil spirit made David shudder. And everyone knew the law in Israel. When someone was possessed by an evil spirit, he was not allowed to live in Israel—he had to leave.

With one eye on the sheep and the other on his target, David took aim and sent another stone flying into a hole in a tree. Difficult questions flooded his mind. *If people with evil spirits are not allowed in Israel, what does this mean for King Saul? Should the king be allowed to reign anymore? Should he have to leave his throne and the country too?*

David had been away from the royal court for over a month now, but he remembered the bad days in the throne room. He remembered a look he often saw on the king's face, a look of desperation and anger and pitiful sadness. The king looked as if he hadn't a friend in the world, and David felt sorry for him. David often wondered what the king was thinking, but he dared not ask. Other times, the look on the king's face gave David a prickling sensation up and down his neck. It was the same feeling he had when he sensed a predator was about to attack his sheep.

The afternoon sun crawled westward. David jumped from his perch on a rocky ledge and called for the sheep. No use worrying about the king or the royal court. Right now, the king was far away on some battlefield. Or not. Probably the whole thing was another false alarm. Probably everyone was already back home, and no one had bothered to come out and tell David the good news.

"One, two, three, four." David counted the sheep as he led them one by one through a narrow opening into a small canyon. The canyon wasn't as safe for the sheep as the open country, but it did have several sheltered spots with greener grass. The days were longer now—David figured he and the sheep could take the risk if it was broad daylight.

David sat down on a stone ledge to watch the sheep graze. He pulled out his knife and began to whittle a wooden whistle. His thoughts went back to the night of the anointing when he and the prophet Samuel had met out by the stables. It all seemed like a faint dream from long ago and far away. The prophet had said

David was the chosen one. What did he mean by that? Was David going to be a village elder in Bethlehem? Was he going to become an officer in the king's army, or perhaps even work as an advisor in the court of the king?

David looked up at the afternoon sky, now blue as hyssop. *Just tell me what You want me to do, God. Tell me what You want me to be. I don't know the first thing about being a leader in Israel. I'm just a shepherd boy.*

As the late afternoon sun warmed the still air of the canyon, David's mind drifted to Israel's king again. What must it be like to be a king? It was probably exciting at times, but it had to be scary sometimes too. All those decisions to make, and those battles to fight—and if things went wrong, the king had to fix the problems or else take the blame.

David pulled his feet up on the ledge and leaned against a rock. *Who really needs a king anyway, when the God of the universe is Israel's Ruler?* As far as David was concerned, no man should be king in Israel. Honestly, David wished it could be like it was in the old days before Israel got a king. He didn't remember those days because he was too young, but his father and mother often talked about what it was like back then. The prophet Samuel had been the spiritual leader of Israel, and each tribe and village was in charge of its own business. Village elders made all the decisions, and there were no taxes, only offerings at the holy sanctuary services at Nob.

David took a long drink from his water skin. He wanted to give the sheep time to eat some of the greener grasses in the canyon, but for some reason, the place made him nervous. Maybe he should move the sheep out of the canyon. Who knew what lurked within its walls!

For a fleeting moment the words to one of David's songs came to mind. "Even when I walk through the darkest valley, I will not be afraid, for You are close beside me." David liked the words, and he liked the way they made him feel. There was no need to be afraid. God was right there beside him.

"Come, Ezra!" David called. "Come, Sheba!" Each sheep had a name, and David knew them all. The sheep always came more quickly when he called them by name.

It took David a few minutes to get the sheep moving in the right direction. The canyon stretched through a rocky pass for several hundred paces. Somewhere in that space of time David began to feel a prickly sensation running down the back of his neck as if someone or something was watching them. Several times David turned sharply, sensing that something was near, but all he saw were a few mountain flowers and a lone hawk sitting in a tree.

David turned to lead the way again, but as he did, he caught sight of a movement far up the canyon. Instantly, David knew they were probably walking right into a trap. Predators were evidently on the prowl again.

David tried to plan what he should do. The afternoon's slanting rays were growing longer. He could retreat the way they had come, but they were probably being stalked from that direction too. No matter what he did, they were going to be ambushed. He wished he knew how many predators there were, but that was the trick, wasn't it?

Beads of sweat began to gather on David's forehead. Whatever he did would have to be aggressive and quick. If he stayed where he was, he might be able to fight off the predators with his sling—at least during daylight. After dark was another matter.

A plan began to form in his mind. It would take daring courage and it would be risky, but it just might work. David bowed his head. *Please Lord! Help me to protect these sheep! I can't do it without You!*

"Come, Ezra!" David called again. "Come, Jochebed! Here, Jezebel and Sheba. Gather round." David circled the flock of sheep into a tight band around the lambs and then commanded, "Hold, Ezra! Hold!" The old ram pressed tightly into the flock, and all the ewes followed his example.

Then, slowly and silently David began to melt into the rocky wall of the canyon as he climbed up and over its face. Leaving his flock was the craziest thing he had ever done, but at the moment, it seemed like the only thing that would work. Somehow, he must take the predators by surprise, whatever and wherever they were.

David found a spot high on the cliff from which he could watch the flock below. He waited for what seemed like an eternity, and then he saw them. First there was one and then another. Finally he could make out the forms of four wolves stealthily creeping into the canyon from opposite directions—two from each end. Their sleek gray coats glistened beautifully in the slanting rays of the sun, but David knew their sharp teeth would slash and cut like knives.

The wolves knew exactly what they were doing. It was an ambush as David had figured, and to anyone watching, it would have looked like disaster for the flock.

Please, Lord! David begged. *Help me make this work! I've got to make this work!* Patiently he waited for the right moment, until one pair of wolves below had crept past him on their way up into the canyon toward the flock of sheep—and then he went into action. David put his shoulder against a large boulder, a boulder so large that it took all the strength he had just to move it. With one final lunge, he pushed it out of its place and down the steep sloping wall of the mountain canyon. As it gained speed, it began to jump and bounce into the air. Other boulders began to move with it, and suddenly an avalanche was in the making.

The pair of wolves below heard the rumble and saw the boulders coming. In a panic they turned back to make their escape, but it was too late. Boulders rained down upon them in a torrent of rock and dust.

David loaded his sling for the second attack. The rumbling avalanche had surprised the other two wolves at the upper end of the canyon, but the two crouching wolves had not yet fled.

David took careful aim with his whirling sling and sent a stone down upon the unsuspecting wolves. In that instant the two wolves saw him and turned to make their escape, but it was too late. The flying stone caught one of the wolves squarely in the shoulder and sent the other one scrambling off to join the rest of the pack. David last caught sight of the straggling wolf pack as they clambered up over the rocky bluffs toward the Engedi wilderness and the Salt Sea.

David stopped to catch his breath and to breathe a prayer of thanksgiving. With God on his side, things always worked out better than he could imagine.

Around the campfire that evening, David cared for the wounds of some of the sheep. Many in the flock had panicked. Two had tried to scramble up the edge of the steep embankment and had fallen back to the canyon floor. Sheba had run into a thorny thicket and cut her leg badly. David poured olive oil on the wounds and bound them up with strips of cloth. "Those briars are nasty, aren't they, Sheba." David patted Sheba's head and sent her back to the flock.

I must get a dog to help with this job, sighed David as he sat down by the fire. Good sheep dogs were hard to find. He wished that he could forget Zeke, their old sheep dog. Zeke was gone. He had died the year before during the cold winter months. There was no doubt about it—Zeke had been the best. No one could handle the sheep like Zeke.

David threw another piece of wood on the fire. He wrapped his cloak around him as the night sounds serenaded him and the sheep. David loved the chirping and buzzing of insects in the grass and the whistle of nighthawk wings high in the sky. He loved the sound of the wind as it sighed its way through the mountain strongholds. To David it was all so peaceful.

"Well, Ezra," David said more to himself than to the ram, "I wonder how much longer I'm going to be out here doing this job." He glanced over his shoulder at the flock of sheep now bedded down in a cave. "I'll tell you what, old boy. I'll make a deal with you—if you'll stick around, I will."

David poked a stick into the fire, sending a shower of sparks upward. Promises! What good was making promises? Even if the old ram lived for many more years, would it really matter? If the Philistines kept moving farther and farther inland, soon there would be no place left for David and his people to live. They'd all have to retreat to the mountains to live with the sheep!

And then there was Abi. David found himself thinking more and more about her. He wondered where she was. Had she fled the village with the others? Had the Philistines already marched on Bethlehem and all of Judah as many had said they would?

David sighed and got out his lyre. It was time to stop thinking about such things. He had a job to do guarding sheep out in the hills. He was just going to have to let God take care of everything else.

THE SECRET PASSAGEWAY

The early morning air was fresh and invigorating when David led the sheep to a nearby mountain spring. Other wild creatures were there already drinking the clear, cold water seeping out of a crack in the stony ground. Two turtledoves sipped the water cautiously, all the while eyeing David and his flock as they approached the spring. A large hare hopped away when he saw David. "I won't hurt you, little one," David said gently. He loved the creatures of the wild—at least the ones that didn't prey on other more helpless animals.

After leading the sheep to a grassy hill to graze, David sat down for an early morning meal. A few handfuls of parched grain and some dried figs seemed enough to satisfy his hunger for the time being. He had set a snare the night before, and he expected he would be eating a quail or partridge for his noonday meal.

The morning passed uneventfully. The average day for a shepherd was boring and even tedious. Watching sheep graze didn't offer much excitement for David, but he didn't waste his time doing nothing or sitting around complaining about it.

There were things he could do, such as tanning the hides from the wolves he had killed a few nights before. The skins were too small to be used as coverings to sleep under, but he could always make a vest or coat to wear. Then, too, he could make several pair of warm foot coverings to wear on the stony paths of the mountain trails. Sometimes David just ran barefoot, but during the winter months or when he was passing through rocky and thorny areas, it helped to put something on his feet.

And of course David always had time to play his lyre. Sometimes when he focused on playing the instrument, the day just seemed to fly away on wings. David knew he had to be careful not to forget what he was supposed to be doing. Playing the lyre always calmed the sheep, but if he lost track of time, there was always going to be a straggler or two that would wander away while he played.

Near noon David heard the distant tones of a ram's horn. He reached for his own horn and blew two long blasts. He hoped it was Joab and Abishai. After taking their mother and sisters to safety weeks before, they had been going back and forth from Hebron to Bethlehem with supplies. Their father needed help with the farm, and, of course, they were always on the lookout for approaching armies.

David waited a few minutes and then blew his horn again. The answering blasts were much closer. Sure enough, before long, Joab and Abishai came walking up the Kidron Valley.

"Hey! Shepherd man! Have you got any room for two weary travelers? We've traveled far, and our stomachs are empty." Joab grinned. "May we sit by your fire and eat from your cooking pot?"

David grinned at his two friends. He never thought of Joab and Abishai just as family, though they actually were his nephews. To him they were also the best of friends.

"Sure, come sit here with me and have something to eat. I have no fire at the moment, but I have some food. I caught a partridge in one of my snares this morning, so we'll have a feast. Did you bring any food with you?"

"We sure did." Joab held up a cloth sack. "Mother gave us a leg of lamb and some pomegranates."

"All right then, let's have a feast."

The boys thanked God for His goodness and for the food. It wasn't a banquet, but to boys camping out, it might as well have been.

David patted his stomach as he sat leaning against a rock. "That sure tasted good! Thanks for sharing your food with me." He sighed. "I'm sure glad you boys came along. It's nice to talk to *people* once in a while—I get pretty tired of talking to the sheep." David laughed. "Now, if you two will spell me for a few minutes, maybe I can catch a few winks."

Bees buzzed back and forth among the field thistles, testing the sweetness of first one and then another. The peace and tranquility of the moment was almost heavenly.

"You want to have some fun a little later on?" David asked sleepily. "There are some pretty neat caves outside the wall of the Jebus fortress. It would be fun to poke around down there for a while." David turned over and closed his eyes. "Oh, and if you want to taste some really good water, there's a spring down inside one of the caves." David licked his lips. "Next to the Bethlehem well water, it's the best I've ever tasted."

Joab took a pomegranate from his shoulder pack and struck it against a rock. "Sure, why not," he said as he sucked some of the ruby red seeds out of the fruit and chewed on their tangy sweetness.

Abishai's eyes lit up. "I'm all for it, but let's go now. Why wait? It's no fun sitting around here watching you two doze off." He squinted at David and Joab in the bright sunlight and then jumped down off the rocky ledge he was sitting on. "Come on! You two can sleep later tonight." Abishai nudged Joab and David with his foot. "We should be able to make it down there with plenty of time to explore the caves before dusk, and then we'll just camp in the caves around there for the night."

David opened his sleepy eyes and shook his head. "Me and my big mouth!" he said with a sigh as he dragged himself to his feet. "Oh, all right. I'm probably never going to get any sleep around here with you jabbering anyway."

During the afternoon hours the three boys took the flock down the Kidron Valley. It wasn't far to the city. They took it slowly so that the older and weaker sheep in the flock wouldn't be worn out. The lambs were big enough to scamper around now.

When the boys arrived at the caves, David and Joab climbed down inside the cave to the spring and drank their fill. "Hey! You're right, this is good water." Joab filled one of his water skins.

"What'd I tell you? It's the best!" David grinned. He studied the walls of the cavern around them. "Now, shall we do a little of that exploring?"

Joab looked up and out through the cave opening. "Sounds good to me. Hey! Abishai! Do you mind watching the sheep for a little while? We're going to check these caves out for a bit!"

"All right!" Abishai called down into the cave. "But I want my turn too."

The two began wading through the pool of water at the bottom of the cave. "I like exploring new caves," David said. "There's nothing like it, because you never know what you're going to find." In the dim light filtering down through the cave opening, David could barely make out Joab's face. "I guess we need a light. We'll have to make a torch or something."

David came back up out of the water. He rummaged in his pack and pulled out a piece of old cloth that he kept for bandaging sheep wounds. He tore off a narrow strip from the cloth and wound it around the end of his rod. Then, he struck a flint against a rock, and sparks jumped onto the cloth of his makeshift torch.

When the sparks began to smolder, David blew on them, and finally the cloth caught fire.

With the lighted torch between them, the two boys walked up through the winding tunnels of the caverns. Suddenly Joab looked up. "Hey, look at this!" He craned his neck to get a better view. "Looks like a shaft cut right into the rock, doesn't it?"

"Sure does." David scratched his head. "I wonder. Hey! Do you think that maybe this is a shaft that goes up through the rock right into the city of Jebus?"

"Could be. Let's climb up and see." Joab found a good foothold and began to inch his way up the face of the shaft. "You'd better tear some more strips off that cloth, so we can have some more light." Joab disappeared from sight up above and then came climbing back down again after several minutes. He was breathing hard.

"It's an entrance to the city, all right. There's an opening up there with a metal grate on it. From where I was, I could see people walking around."

David nodded his head. "Hmm, sounds like they've fixed it up so that they can come down here and get water when the city is under siege or something." He tied another strip of cloth on the torch to keep it burning and then glanced up the shaft. "Did anybody see you while you were up there?"

"I don't know. Maybe. Soldiers were looking toward the metal grate over the opening. I think we'd better get out of here before someone catches us and we really get in trouble."

"Good idea." David lifted the flickering torch high over his head. "Besides, our supply of cloth is running out—our torch is going to go out if we don't hurry. Then we'll really have a hard time finding our way out of here."

When the two boys finally climbed out of the cave again, darkness was settling over the countryside. Abishai had taken the sheep up to the top of a ridge overlooking the fortress. He had corralled the sheep in a small cave and had a fire going.

Around the fire later that night, the boys ate some barley loaves and the last of the roasted lamb Joab and Abishai had brought with them. Joab and Abishai wanted David to play his lyre for them, but David was so tired he just lay down and covered himself with his mantle.

"Hey, boys!" he yawned sleepily. "That was fun in the caves this afternoon. Sorry you didn't get a chance to explore too, Abishai."

"Oh, that's all right. From the sound of it, it's not safe being in there anyway." Abishai shook his head. "I wonder how many other people know about that secret passageway into the fortress of Jebus."

David pulled his mantle tighter around his shoulders. "I doubt many people know about it, or the Jebusites would be in trouble."

"Yeah, well, if we ever want to conquer the city of Jebus, that secret passageway would be a great place to start." Joab's laugh sounded nervous. "But tomorrow we'd better move on before they find us out here and get suspicious."

David yawned again. "You know, if I were ever a king, I'd want to have a fortress like Jebus for my capital. It would be great! It's built on a mountaintop, it's got a secret water supply, and it has a great escape tunnel in case of an emergency." David opened his eyes and grinned at Joab. "And you could be my general. What do you think?"

"I think you're out of your mind, shepherd boy." Joab put another piece of wood on the fire and shook his head. "You'd make a great king, but I guess I shouldn't say such things. We can't have another king in Israel—we've already got one. Go to sleep, David."

David stared into the fire. It was hard to listen to Joab talk like that and not tell him everything, but David knew it wasn't wise at this time to tell anyone about what the prophet Samuel had said. Everything would come together in due time. For now, the whole thing must still remain a secret. Hadn't he and Abi made a pact to tell no one? David smiled. Abi was a pretty sensible for a girl her age. And wise too.

The fire felt good on David's face. He yawned again and closed his eyes. For now he just wanted to sleep. He knew he deserved it, whether he was a shepherd boy or a king.

BATTLE OF THE BANDITS

Sometime during the night, Abishai woke David and asked him to take the third watch. Joab had taken the first watch, so Abishai must have taken the second.

David splashed his face with cool water to wake up and then climbed into a crevice in the rocks above the cave where the sheep were bedded down. The fire had died down because there was no more wood at hand, but a full moon lit up the Kidron Valley as it slowly set in the western sky. David looked across the valley at the fortress of Jebus standing tall and silent atop the hill of Zion, or Mount Zion, as some called it. Even in the dark, he could see the silhouettes of the sentries standing on the wall of the fortress.

David smiled to himself in the darkness. The fortress was in a perfect location. It would be impossible to scale those walls, even if an army could climb the steep banks to reach them. With all its advantages, he was sure the city of Jebus would be a perfect place for a capital city in the kingdom of Israel.

He began to think about his conversation with Joab from the night before. Was it possible that the prophet had been thinking about David as a future king of Israel? The idea seemed far-fetched, and David wasn't sure he should be entertaining such an idea. The very idea made him shiver with both excitement and fear, but if that's what the prophet Samuel had in mind, David wondered when it would be. Five years? Ten years? Twenty? The idea of being king someday was a scary thought. It seemed like a dream that could never ever be real. There were too many pieces of the puzzle that didn't seem to fit. What about King Saul? He would not be happy at having someone like David taking over his throne. He would want one of his own sons to be the next king.

And what about the Philistines? How would they fit into the picture? It was a tragedy that enemies such as the Philistines should be allowed to live in the land of Israel! If David became king some day, would he have to deal with them? Would he be able to overthrow them and run them out of the country, or would they oppress the Israelites forever?

And the Jebusites?

It made David sad to think of all the bad influences these heathen people had on Israel, living right there among them. Idol worship and nonstop wars were problems, and some of the young men were taking wives from the heathen nations. David set his jaw in determination. It was time for God's people to humble themselves and pray! It was time for them to make a commitment for God and for the right! It was time that they all stand up and chase these evil nations out of Israel! This was the Promised Land given to David's ancestors! Why should Israel be afraid to make the Philistines or Jebusites leave the country?

"If no one else is going to make them leave, then I guess I will," David spoke the words right out loud. He laughed to himself in the darkness, realizing that there was no one around to even hear him say such a thing—especially not Joab and Abishai; they were both prety much dead to the world right now.

The stillness of the night pressed in around David. No breeze was blowing. The only sounds he could hear were the breathing of Joab and Abishai and the twittering of night birds in the trees nearby.

And then suddenly David did hear a sound. It was the footsteps of someone coming from the north along a rocky ledge overlooking the Kidron Valley. And voices—more than one voice. David could make out two voices—no, three, or maybe more, and they were coming right his way.

Who could they be? Soldiers from the fortress of Jebus? Robbers? A gang of Moabite bandits roaming the country looking for trouble? David braced himself for an attack. More than likely, whoever was coming knew exactly what David was doing here. They probably knew that he had a flock of sheep with him and only two young boys to help him guard them. And David himself was only two years older than Joab.

The footsteps sounded closer now. There wasn't much time to decide what to do. David could barely make out their crouching shadowy forms as they ducked their way along the ledge from tree to boulder and then to tree again.

"Help me, Lord!" David whispered. "God is our refuge and strength, always ready to help in times of trouble."

Instinctively, David reached into his shepherd's bag and pulled out a smooth round stone. He put it into his sling and grasped the sling tightly. He knew that if he needed to fight these evil men, he'd better be ready to give them the surprise of their lives!

Quickly David's sling was whirling over his head, and in the next instant the stone was crashing into the shadowy form of someone not many paces away. David heard a man's voice cry out in pain, and he knew he had hit his mark. He pulled another stone from his bag and loaded it into his sling. Seconds later another man moaned and stumbled as he half-crawled, half-rolled down the hill into the Kidron Valley.

There were others, but David only heard their footsteps running away. In the morning when Joab and Abishai awoke, they found the footprints of the men. There had been at least six of them. Around a breakfast of figs, cheese, and parched grain, the boys thanked God for His protection the night before.

"How did you fight them off all by yourself?" Abishai asked. "You should have woken me up! I'd have helped take them out one by one."

"Looks like he didn't need any help," laughed Joab. "He probably does this kind of thing all the time."

"That's not true!" David insisted. "Or—well—I mean, the part about me not needing you, at least. You guys know I need you. I do! You help me out more than you'll ever know! If you two didn't come out here now and then, even just to keep me company, I'd go crazy for sure!"

That morning the boys moved the sheep down the Kidron Valley closer to Bethlehem. They knew they'd feel safer farther away from the bandits and the fortress of Jebus.

In the early afternoon, they heard the sound of a ram's horn drifting over the hills from the south. Joab returned the signal with his own horn, and before long Mahlon arrived, panting and out of breath.

"Mahlon! What brings you out here?" David asked. "Is everything all right back home?"

Mahlon smiled between deep breaths of air. "Yes, David. But your father wants you to come home. He has business for you to tend to with your brothers."

"My brothers?" David asked excitedly. "Are Eliab and the others back?"

Mahlon took another deep breath. "Whew! That's a long uphill walk! I'm not as young as I used to be." He smiled at David. "No, your brothers aren't back yet. Actually, your father wants you to take some supplies to the front lines. He's worried about your brothers."

For a moment, David was speechless. Then he blurted, "Me? Father wants to send me to the front lines?"

"That's what he says." Mahlon smiled again knowing how often David had talked of going away to war. "But I think you'd better hurry before he has a chance to change his mind."

"I—I'm going! I'm going!" David shouted excitedly as he hurried to collect his belongings and stuff them into his pack. Suddenly he stopped and looked at Joab and Abishai. He knew they wished they could go too.

"Who's going to look after the sheep, Mahlon?"

Mahlon shook his head. "Don't worry, David, I'm here to cover for you."

"Well, what about them?" David pointed at Joab and Abishai.

"You better take them along too." The corners of Mahlon's mouth twitched ever so slightly. "I heard the men in the village saying that they wanted to send Joab and Abishai along too."

"Yippee!" shouted Joab. "Come on, Abishai! We're going to the front lines, and we're going to give those Philistines a piece of our minds!"

Mahlon shook his head and laughed as the three boys scampered off down the mountain trail. Even when they crested the last hill in the distance, he could see they were still running.

When David and the two boys passed through the gate of Bethlehem, David's father was sitting in judgment with the other village elders. Evidently there were at least some people still in Bethlehem. The elders were seated on benches along the wall just inside the village gate. A man had stolen three goats from his neighbor and was receiving sentence. The three boys stopped for a few moments to watch, and their mouths dropped open in surprise. The accused was none other than Shimei.

"Shimei, son of Gera, according to the law of Moses and of Israel, you are hereby ordered to give your neighbor, Uzzah, four goats for each goat you have taken." David's father was the spokesman and evidently in charge of the trial. "That will be a total of twelve goats, Shimei, because you stole three."

"But—but, that isn't fair!" Shimei sputtered. "The law of Moses clearly states that I need return only double!"

Jesse looked at Shimei sternly. "My son, that is only if the animal is yet in your hands, but this is not the case. You have already sold the animals to an Ishmaelite trader who came through yesterday. Is this not true?"

Shimei hung his head but said nothing.

"Then our decision is final! We hereby sentence you to restore the man his stolen property by sunset tomorrow night, or you will be given a more severe penalty!" Jesse looked at Shimei without flinching. "In addition to this, you are also being relieved of your responsibilities on my farm! I cannot have a dishonest man working for me!"

The eight village elders sitting at the gate looked at Shimei grimly, but Shimei did not respond. He only turned and walked away without speaking.

David, Joab, and Abishai quietly left the village gate and walked on into the village until they were out of earshot.

"I knew it!" David announced. "I told my father that Shimei couldn't be trusted as a servant! Maybe now he'll believe me when I give him advice about men he wants to hire!"

"What do think Shimei will do?" Abishai asked. "Will he pay the price?"

"Oh, he'll pay the price! He has to—but he'll hold a grudge. And if I know Shimei, he'll find a way someday to get back at my father!" David frowned. "And if he can't get back at my father, he'll probably find a way to get back at me!"

"Where's he from?" Joab shifted his pack to his other shoulder.

"He's from Bahurim, in the territory of Benjamin. His father's name is Gera, and the family is related to King Saul."

Joab frowned. "Uh-oh! This doesn't sound good. If he is from the king's family, what is he doing here in Bethlehem?"

"Uhh, there was some trouble in the village of Bahurim, I think. No one knows for sure, but I heard that Shimei's own father won't even speak to him."

"OK, guys!" Abishai interrupted David and Joab's conversation. "We have more important things to think about right now. If we want to reach the battlefield tomorrow, we're going to have to get an early start in the morning! Come on, Joab! Let's go!"

* * *

Before the sun had streaked the dawn with pink, orange, and yellow, David and his friends were up and loading their donkeys. Joab and Abishai and several other boys from Bethlehem arrived at David's house before David had even finished eating his morning meal.

"I'm glad you're going, my son." David's father stood by as Huldah helped David load his donkey. "We haven't heard from the front lines for so long now that I'm sending you with some bread, dried fruit, and a sack of parched grain. Your brothers will like that—I hope it lasts them a while." Jesse smiled. "It's good that Huldah is back. She arrived yesterday to help us get all this stuff ready."

David's father turned to go and then paused. "Oh! And I'm also sending you with a gift of ten round cheeses for Eliab's superior officer. See that he gets them, David."

"Don't worry, Father. We'll give him the gift as soon as we get there."

David grabbed the lead rope of his donkey. "Come on, boys, we've got to get going." The boys quickly headed toward the gate.

"Mind if I walk a ways with you?" David turned suddenly at the sound of Abi's voice.

"Abi! What are you doing here?" he asked in surprise.

"Oh, I was up helping my brother get packed to go, and I thought I might just slip over here and see you off. You'll be careful, won't you?" Abi looked worried.

"Yeah, we'll be OK. We've got our slings and our knives and even some food. We're all ready for war, aren't we, boys?" The boys all laughed together.

Abi frowned. "I'm serious, David! A battlefield is not a place for games! These Philistines are out for blood—and they'll take it, too, if you let them!"

David's face grew serious. "You're right, Abi, but for so long now I've wanted to see the Philistines and even fight them. I guess I just forgot to be afraid."

Tears welled up in Abi's eyes. "I'm afraid, David! Our soldiers have been there for so long now, and no one has sent word back about any of the battles!" Abi sniffed through her tears. "The rumors say that they have a surprise weapon, a man who can fight like lions!"

"I know, I've heard that too, but we don't need to be worried, Abi. If God is for us, who can be against us?" David reassured her. "We'll be all right, Abi!" He smiled shyly at her. "Now, you'd better be getting back—it's still dark out here on the road."

David hurried to catch up with the others. "Hey, Joab! Abishai! I know a shortcut that will get us there much quicker. It goes south of the Valley of Rephaim and up over the hills near Manahath. . . ."

And with that the boys and their pack animals disappeared into the shadows of the early dawn.

A SURPRISE WEAPON

David stood on a bluff with the boys from Bethlehem, staring out over the Valley of Elah. "I can't believe we're here!" he shouted. "We're really here!"

Below them, the boys could see the entire battlefield. On one side of a large ravine was the Israelite camp. It was perched on a sloping hill that was bordered by trees on the north side and the south. The Philistine camp was across the deep ravine on another range of hills. The tents of the Philistine army were colorful—reds and greens and blues. A frown crossed David's face. To him it looked like there were a lot more Philistine soldiers than Israelite ones.

"Just look at that Philistine camp!" Abishai was so excited. "Isn't it something! Hey! It looks like they're getting ready for a battle or something! Come on, guys! Let's get down there! I want to get as close as I can to see all the action!"

Joab grabbed the lead rope of Abishai's donkey. "Wait a minute!" He ordered. "We came here with all this food and stuff, and we're supposed to makes sure our brothers and fathers get it, so let's do that before we do anything else!" Joab shook his head unbelievingly and turned to the rest of the boys. "And watch yourself, all of you! This isn't a feast day! It's a battlefield where people kill each other any day of the week! There's a war going on down there!"

The boys led their donkeys down the steep hill to the valley below, and then to the supply captain of the Israelite army. They left their provisions with him and then asked where they could find the men from Bethlehem.

David found his brothers near the rear of the Israeli troops. "Abinadab! Shammah!" he shouted excitedly as he ran to where they were making last-minute preparations for the battle. "I brought you some food from home—some of Huldah's good bread and parched grain and other stuff!"

Abinadab took one look at David and scowled. "What are you doing here, David? You can't come down to the battle-field like this! It's not safe! And is that Joab and Abishai I see over there?" Abinadab shook his head. "This is no place for kids! Do Father and the other parents know you boys are here?"

"Of course Father knows we're here!" David glanced at Joab and Abishai. "What did you think, that we snuck down here all on our own!"

"I wouldn't be a bit surprised, with the kind of stunts you try to pull!" Abinadab replied. "Anyway, you don't belong here, David, whether Father sent you or not!"

Shammah stepped up to David. "That's right! If he knew how serious the situation is here, he never would have sent you!" Shammah pointed back the way David had come. "Now get off the battlefield!"

David was stunned. How could his brothers treat him like this? It wasn't right. The injustice of it all made him angry. He was embarrassed and he was humiliated, but he knew he shouldn't have been surprised. Always it was the same.

In disappointment David turned to go, when suddenly a shout was raised from across the ravine to the west. An echo of deafen-ing cheers rose on the morning air, and the clang of metal on metal could be heard up and down the entire valley. Unfortu-nately, the noise was all coming from across the ravine in the Philistine camp.

David found an empty supply cart and climbed into it. As his sharp eyes scanned the Philistine army gathering into battle formation across the ravine, a cold shiver suddenly shot up and down his spine! There, coming across the open space of ground at the front of the Philistine army, was a huge hulk of a man, a soldier dressed from head to foot in the latest of Philistine armor! David's mouth dropped open. He was big! He had to be, because the soldiers standing next to him looked like midgets! Or so it seemed. David gulped—was the giant a real man?

He was carrying a gigantic spear, and metal plates of armor covered his entire chest! A giant sword was strapped to his side, and on his huge head he wore a helmet with red feathers sticking out of the top!

David suddenly realized that he had been holding his breath. "Whew! Joab! Look at the size of that man! He's got to be half again as tall as a grown man! A lot taller even than King Saul, and the king's a head taller than anyone in the Israelite army!" David shook his head in disbelief.

Joab climbed up into the cart beside David and grabbed David's arm. He looked scared. "I can't believe it!" he croaked. "I've never seen anyone so big in all my life!"

"Me neither! I've heard about these guys, but I never thought I'd feel this way when I actually saw one of them!" David put his hands to his head. "This man's got to be what's left over from the giants that lived in the land when our great-great-grandfathers first came here hundreds of years ago!"

"Yeah—sons of Anak, maybe?"

"Probably." David just stood with his mouth open. "How many of them do you think the Philistine army has?"

"Who knows!" Joab stared at the giant now striding back and forth on the other side of the ravine. "They probably only need the one! How tall do you think he is?"

"Oh—six cubits, I'd say. Maybe more!" David cringed. "But it doesn't matter, Joab! That giant might as well be seven or eight cubits!" David laughed nervously. "Hey! He might as well be a hundred cubits for all the difference it makes!"

"So what are we going to do?" Joab was shaking.

"I don't know!" David glanced over at Abishai. Not much usually scared Abishai. He was brave in a stubborn sort of way, and sometimes he rushed headlong into things without really counting the cost or risk. But right now his mouth was hanging open too, and even he looked scared!

"You know, David, I think Abinadab and Shammah are probably right. This is no place for boys! We should probably leave!" Joab was serious. "I mean, really—we brought the stuff our families sent us with. We've done our job. This doesn't look good, and it could get pretty ugly, here, if—"

But Joab was suddenly interrupted as the morning air was shattered by a voice so big and powerful that it made David shake right down to the tips of his toes.

"Good morning, Hebrew children! Did you sleep well last night?" The Philistine soldiers in the front ranks broke into laughter, and the rippling effect spread out over their entire army. The ground seemed to shake under the giant's feet as he walked to the edge of the rocky ravine and shook his fist. "King Saul!" he shouted, "Come out, come out, wherever you are!"

The Israelite army had been holding their ground until now, but at the sound of the giant's voice, they broke ranks and began to retreat to the Israelite camp!

The giant began to laugh uproariously. "King Saul!" he shouted. "Your men are such cowards! Look at them run, and why shouldn't they? With nothing but a miserable, no-good, feeble excuse for a king, what do you expect! You're the king of cowards!"

The giant slapped his knee with one of his huge hands and began to laugh again. "Well, King Saul! I'm offering you a chance again this morning! Send me a real man who will fight your battles for you! If he can strike me down, then Israel will have won the battle, and we will be your slaves forever!" The giant began to laugh in fiendish delight. "But," he roared, "if I win in the fight against your man, then you will be our slaves!" The giant pounded the ground with the butt of his spear as he continued to laugh. "Is there no man in Israel who will accept this challenge?"

But King Saul did not come out of the large tent his generals had set up as a command post. David could only imagine what they were doing in there. Did they have a secret strategy that they were about to unleash? Did they have a weapon of their own that they hoped would defeat the giant?

The giant's voice grew louder. "For forty days now I have come morning and evening to offer you a chance to gain back your dignity! What ails you, King Saul?" The giant cleared his throat and then spat into the ravine between the armies. "I'll tell you what your problem is! Your problem is that you are weak! You are pathetically weak, and your God is weak!" The giant snorted, and then cursed the God of Israel. "Your God can't deliver you from us! He's probably dead, and even if He is alive, He's not strong enough. You pitiful Israelites are living proof of that!"

David caught his breath. How could this man say these horrible things? To curse Israel and even King Saul was bad enough, but to curse God, the Creator of heaven and earth, was too frightening to even think about! It didn't matter that this man was a giant! Giant or not, no one had the right to arrogantly stand up against the God of Israel! Hadn't these people ever heard the stories of how Pharaoh's pride was humbled when God sent the ten plagues on Egypt? Hadn't they heard how God had parted the Red Sea so that Israel could pass through and escape from Pharaoh's army? Hadn't anyone told these Philistines about what happened to the evil nations, right here in the land of Canaan, when Israel had taken the land by storm? Evidently not.

David gritted his teeth. "Joab, I'm not standing for this any longer. This is a wicked man with nothing but evil mischief planned for God's people. God doesn't like it, I don't like it, and I can't imagine that King Saul is happy about it, either!"

Joab stared at David. "Well—OK, but what can you do about it?"

David jumped down from the cart. "I don't know, but I'll think of something!"

THE CHALLENGE

"Sir!" David stepped up to tall soldier standing next to the cart and pointed at the giant standing across the ravine to the west. "Who does this man think he is that he can defy the God of heaven and insult our king! And where does he get the right to curse Israel!"

The soldier looked at David and then pointed at the giant who was pacing back and forth, ranting and raving. "He's Goliath, that's who he is!"

David was unimpressed. "That may be, but what makes him think that he can act like this and get away with it!"

"Are you crazy?" The soldier stared at David in disbelief. "He's a giant—or haven't you noticed!"

"That doesn't make any difference," David insisted, "or at least it shouldn't!"

The soldier looked annoyed, but he finally just grunted and decided to ignore David.

Joab hopped down off the cart and walked to David's side. "Come on, David! I don't think this is such a good idea."

David brushed Joab aside. "I don't get it!" He persisted. "Isn't anybody going to go out there and fight the giant?" David turned to several other soldiers standing nearby. "How can you all just stand around and let him talk like that! He's given out the challenge, and he's cussing and swearing besides!"

A big burly soldier turned to glare at David. "Listen, kid! If you know what's good for you, you'll get out of here!"

David couldn't believe his ears. "Oh, come on! There's got to be a man brave enough and strong enough in the army of Israel to get out there and fight the giant! There's just got to be!" He squinted at the soldiers standing all around. "And besides, the Lord is on our side! He will deliver the giant into our hands! With God all things are possible!"

Two other soldiers finally came over to where David was standing. "Who do you think you are, kid? And what gives you the right to come around here and preach to us about bravery? We don't need that kind of talk right now! You're just a kid." The two soldiers' eyes looked afraid. "And what are you doing here, anyway?" they added. "Battlefields are for men, not for boys!"

David's eyes flashed. "Hey! I may be a boy, but I'm not afraid! And I'm sixteen anyway! That's not so young! I can fight! I've handled lions and bears before! They're not so bad!" David was fairly sputtering by now.

One of the soldiers jerked his head in the direction of the giant. "Yeah, well, the giant is going back to the Philistine camp now, so you don't need to worry about it, anyway!"

Another soldier walked up to David and patted him on the head as though he were a little boy. "Go home to your mama," he said with a half smile.

David pushed the soldier's hand away impatiently. "I'm not afraid to fight the giant!" he shouted. David tried to control himself, but felt like he wanted to lash out in anger.

Joab grabbed David's arm. "Come on, David. You're starting to make these soldiers mad. You don't want to get us into trouble, do you?"

"Trouble!" David snapped. "How could we get into any worse trouble than we're already in? The nation of Israel is caving in because we all stand around and let a Philistine soldier blaspheme the Lord of hosts! Now, that's trouble, if you ask me!"

A crowd of soldiers began to gather around David. "Save your breath!" said a soldier with a jagged scar on his cheek. "Next, I suppose you'll be telling us you want to fight this giant all by your little lonesome self!"

"That's right!" another sneered. "And I suppose he thinks he's going to fight the giant so he can collect the bounty from the king!"

"Yeah, and he's going to marry the king's daughter as a reward for his valiant bravery in battle!" The soldiers were really getting rowdy now! They were so stirred up that it was almost as if they had forgotten to be afraid of Goliath!

Suddenly the crowd of soldiers split as Eliab came striding through. "What's going on here?" he exclaimed. He took one look at David and shouted, "I knew it! I just knew that somehow you'd eventually find a way to get down here!" Eliab shook his head as he spotted Joab and Abishai. "It wasn't enough that you had to trick Father into letting you come and see the battle—you had to go and bring a bunch of other kids with you, too! You should be ashamed of yourself, David! Making mother sick with worry, and who'd you leave the sheep with, anyway?"

David was speechless. What could he say? He hadn't asked to come to the battlefield—Father had sent him. He had just followed orders to bring some good home cooking to his brothers, and this was the way they treated him! David was crushed! All the anger he kept inside began to well up. All the resentment he had felt toward his brothers, and especially Eliab, came out in a flood now.

"What did I do to deserve this?" David spoke in low tones through clenched teeth. "And why is it that you always have to treat me like a little child, Eliab? Aren't I good enough to be your brother? You'd think we weren't even from the same family!"

Eliab turned red in the face. He ignored David's protest, and turned to go. "Get your things and get out of here!" he ordered. "And don't let me catch you sneaking around here again!"

David stood his ground. He wanted to be respectful to Eliab, but he figured if he ever wanted to gain some respect, it was now or never. "I'm not going." David said the words calmly, and with determination in his voice, "If no one else will fight the giant, then I will."

A silence settled over the group of soldiers.

Eliab stopped dead in his tracks. "You?" he almost spat the words out.

"That's right!" David added. "If no one else is going to stand up to this raving maniac who dares to curse the king and even God Himself, then I will. It's wrong for the giant to do this, and someone needs to teach him a lesson!"

David took a deep breath. There. He had said what was on his mind, and it felt good. He knew there would probably be a price to pay, but it didn't matter anymore. He felt that he had done the right thing.

"You!" Eliab repeated, as he shook his head in disbelief. "I'm going to pretend I didn't hear you say that!"

David looked Eliab squarely in the eye, but didn't say a word.

Eliab glanced around nervously and snorted. "This has got to be some kind of a joke!"

No one moved, and not a soldier opened his mouth. What was there to say? The unexpected had happened. Someone had offered to face the huge giant, and even though it was a boy, it took guts to do that! He deserved their respect—it was something none of them had had the courage to do. Even if the boy didn't actually get to go out and fight the giant, it had taken courage to stand up and say he would do it.

Eliab laughed right out loud as he stared at the soldiers crowded around. "You're not listening to this, are you?" he asked in amazement. "This is my brother! This is David, the little one—

the youngest! He's just a kid!" Eliab was growing more impatient by the second. "Do you know what this boy does at home for the family? He watches the sheep! He watches the sheep!" Eliab repeated the words for emphasis and snorted again. "He's not going out to fight this giant! Not now! Not ever! He's got no experience as a soldier! He's just a boy!"

Suddenly the crowd of soldiers split again as two heavily armed guards stepped up to David. "Are you the one who said he wants to fight the giant?"

David stared at the two guards in surprise, and then at Joab and Abishai. He looked at Eliab, but Eliab only shrugged his shoulders and shook his head in disgust.

David didn't flinch. "Yes, that's me."

"Then come with us!" was all they would say.

MAN OF THE HOUR

"Step this way, boy." A guard opened a flap to the entrance of the large goatskin tent the king was using as a military command post.

David glanced at Joab still beside him.

"You're crazy, David!" Joab said worriedly.

Inside the tent, David had to pause while his eyes adjusted to the darkness. At the back of the tent, two torches burned brightly, held by soldiers standing guard on either side of a makeshift throne. But the king was not sitting on his throne.

A large papyrus map covered a table in the corner. The flickering light from oil lamps on the table only dimly illuminated the faces of those huddled around the table. After David's eyes adjusted to the darkness, he could still barely make out the faces of several military officers and—the king himself.

David dropped to one knee. Again he was in the presence of his king. He forgot that he should be afraid of this man who sometimes acted like a raving lunatic. He forgot his anger at his brothers, and especially Eliab, for treating him like a child. David didn't know what to expect or why exactly he had been called into the command post, but he did know that he was in the presence of the Lord's anointed, and that was all that mattered. More than anything else, David wanted to serve his king and his God.

The men around the table turned at the sound of David's entrance. "What's he doing here?" one of the generals demanded.

The guard snapped to attention, his spear standing straight at his side. "He's the one you asked to see, sir."

The general stood to his feet. His uniform was impressive even in the dim lamp light. His military tunic was fastened tightly by a wide leather belt. A breastplate covered his chest, a red sash was draped over his shoulder, and he held his helmet in the crook of his arm. However, his face looked as hard as stone.

"He's just a boy!" The general looked angry. "Where's the man you said offered to fight the giant?"

The soldier at attention looked nervous. "This is the one, sir!"

The general turned back to the table in disgust. "Well, we can't have a boy going out there! This is preposterous! I thought you were talking about an experienced soldier!" The general dismissed them with a wave of his hand. "Take him away!"

The general turned back to the table as David rose from his knee and stepped to the door of the tent. The king watched David go, and as the tent flap opened, he caught a glimpse of David's face.

"David, my boy! It's you!" The king stood to his feet in surprise as he suddenly recognized David. "It is so good to see you again!" the king added. He sighed as though a great weight were pressing down on him.

David turned and again dropped to one knee. "As always, I am at your service, my king."

"Yes, of course. Come here, son." The king beckoned to David to join him and his military officers around the table. He studied David's face carefully. "Is what they say true, David?"

David kept his head bowed while in the presence of the king. "You mean about my offer to fight the giant?"

"Yes."

"I *am* willing to fight the giant, my lord." David spoke slowly and respectfully. "But even though I have fought wilderness battles against bands of roving bandits and Moabite raiders, I have never fought in your army, sir."

"And you wish to fight this Philistine giant?" the king asked skeptically.

David's voice was steady. "I am willing to go out to battle the giant in the name of the Lord. He will help me win the battle for you and for all of Israel."

The king looked worried. "You understand, of course, that if you lose, we will be their slaves?" There was a long pause, and then the king added, "David, my boy, no one wants to be the slave of a Philistine. We would all be better off dead!"

David's chose his words carefully. "I understand, my king, but this is where faith in God's promises must come in. With God's help, we will win this battle today!"

The king turned to his officers and smiled weakly. "He has the heart of a lion, doesn't he? You certainly have to give him credit for bravery."

The officers merely grunted. It was obvious that they thought David was interrupting important military business.

The king noticed David glancing at the diagrams on the sheet of papyrus spread out on the table. There was something about David that drew the king to the boy. He couldn't quite put his finger on it, but it was a strange and unusual self-confidence that the king hadn't seen for a long time.

"Tell me then, my boy, do you think we should use the strategy that the generals have laid out here on this map?" The king pointed to several rows of circles and slash marks on the papyrus and then glanced at the general with the red sash over his shoulder. "General Abner, explain our plan of attack to David."

General Abner glanced at the king, and then at David. "Yes, sir," he said reluctantly in a gravelly voice. "Now, you will notice here on the right flank that we have placed the majority of our troops. They will stand their ground until they receive the signal from my ram's horn. And over here among the hills to the south, we have positioned a small detachment of soldiers under General Zemirah.

"At dawn, under cover of darkness, General Zemirah and his men will sweep into the Philistine camp from the rear and take them by surprise." The general stopped and looked at the king as though waiting for the king to say something.

The king turned to David. "So, David, my boy, what do you think?"

David's face went blank for a few moments, and then he finally found his voice. "I'm sure you don't need my advice, my Lord," he protested.

"But I want it!" King Saul urged. "The boy intrigues me!"

David glanced at the faces of the officers around the table, one by one. He studied the plans on the table for a few moments longer, and then finally spoke. His answer was short and to the point. "My lord, it would seem that many lives would be lost if we use this strategy. Goliath has offered to fight a man of our choice. I think we should take him up on his offer."

"But we have no such man!" snapped General Abner.

The king looked at David again and shook his head sadly. "I know that you think you can do this, my son, and you want to serve your country; but I fear you have no idea what you are up against. This man, Goliath, is nearly twice your size, and he must weigh five or six times what you weigh. He is a ferocious man, a soldier experienced in war from his earliest days!"

The king looked David up and down. "The giant's armor is the best that has ever been made. The coat of mail that covers his chest is made of bronze—our generals estimate that it weighs at least five thousand shekels. He doesn't even carry his own shield. Someone else does that for him, so that he can be free to use other weapons." The king paused. "Let's see. He has a spear that is made of iron. It weighs at least six hundred shekels. And his sword?" The king cleared his throat. "You don't want to know about his sword."

The king sighed again. "So, you see, my son, it is impossible that you could face this man alone and live to tell about it! As you said before, you have no real experience on the battlefield!"

David set his jaw in determination. "I mean no offense, my king, but I think I do have experience. I have battled with wild beasts in the wilderness. While guarding my father's sheep I have killed lions and bears. I have outsmarted entire packs of wolves and have battled with gangs of bandits. Through all this I have never lost a sheep or lamb. I have even had to take the lamb right out of the beast's mouth. The Lord has been with me, my king, and He is the One that has given me the courage to fight for the life of my sheep."

The king stared at David intently as though the boy were his own son. "Tell me, David," the king said, "why do you really want to fight this giant? Is it for the possible reward you might receive from me?"

David took a deep breath. This time he dared to raise his eyes and look directly into the face of the king. "My king, this giant has defied the Lord God of Israel. No one can do this and live!" David slowly shook his head. "The people before the Flood in Noah's day learned that, and so did Pharaoh in ancient Egypt. The city of Jericho fell because of its defiance of our God. In every age, evil people have had to learn that lesson. There is no God like our God in all the earth!" David's voice rang out as though he was inspired. "Our God is a merciful God, but He is also just! We need to face the Philistines today and let them know that the God of Israel will stand up and deliver His people!" David bowed his head again respectfully. "I am sure that God will give us this giant and this victory today, my king."

The king stood to his feet and slowly reached out his hand to David. "Then go, my son, and may the God of Abraham, Isaac, and Jacob go with you."

Turning to General Abner, the king said, "Give David the finest armor you can find."

The general just stared at the king.

The king turned to his throne and then stopped and looked at David. "No, wait a minute! On second thought, let's just give him my armor." The king began to take the pieces of his armor off, one by one. "It's the best we have," he said sadly.

General Abner clapped his hands, and a servant came to assist the king. The breastplate was removed and put on David. It hung down past David's waist. The sword in its sheath was so long it nearly dragged on the ground, and the helmet was a bit too big.

"I don't think this is going to work," David said slowly. "If I wear the helmet, it will come down over my eyes."

The king sighed, "What are we going to do! We can't just let you go out without protection." The king began to look around at what his officers were wearing. "Maybe we can find you another suit of armor that will fit better."

David turned to the king. "Please, my king, may I speak freely?"

"Go ahead," the king replied.

"I want to thank you and your men for all that you have tried to do for me today—but—I can't fight with this heavy armor on." David looked down at the bulky armor. "Please—I'm not sure it would matter whose armor I was wearing. I have not worn armor in battle, so I don't really know how to use it. I'm afraid it will only slow me down."

"Then what will you wear?" the king asked in surprise. "What will you fight with, and how will you be protected?"

David took off the breastplate of mail and the metal shin guards. Handing the king's helmet to Abner, David picked up his shepherd's rod and his sling.

General Abner's mouth dropped open. "What are you going to do with those?" he asked, pointing at the rod and sling.

A strange light came into David's eyes as he looked at the king and his officers standing all around him. "With these two weapons I will fight the giant in God's name, and I will win!"

AN ARMY OF ONE

"This is a silly notion, boy!" General Abner objected. "You can't go out there with only a shepherd's rod and a sling! That giant will cut you up into little pieces before you even know what hit you!" The general turned to the king. "My lord, I knew that this was a bad idea. I knew we should never—"

The king held up his hand for silence. "I'm not so sure you're right, General. If the boy thinks he can kill a giant with a sling, maybe he can." The king then turned to David. "You say you've killed bears and lions and beasts with a sling?"

"Yes, my lord!"

The king looked at his generals one by one. "Then I say we let him try!"

David stood tall and looked at the king with new appreciation in his heart. The king believed in him, and David believed in God's power—that's what really mattered. It didn't matter that his brothers made fun of him and thought of him as only a shepherd boy. It didn't matter that the generals saw him as an inexperienced fighter. The king had faith in him, and that made up for everything else others might think.

David turned to General Abner. "What time will I need to be ready to fight the giant?"

General Abner scratched his beard and sighed. "Goliath comes out every morning before noon. He comes out again in the afternoon, about the ninth hour. Come back here before then."

"Yes, sir," David saluted the general. "I'll be back, but I'd like to see my brothers again first."

As David left the tent, he could hear the king talking to his officers inside. "Does anybody know who this boy is? I know his name is David, and he's been to the court and played his lyre for me several times, but I know almost nothing else about him. Who did you say his father is, and where does he come from . . . ?" The king's voice faded away as David walked out into the sunshine. David squinted while his eyes adjusted to the brightness.

Joab and Abishai were waiting for David outside the door to the command post. "What's going on, David?" Joab asked. "You were in there forever! What did the king say?"

"Come on!" David grinned. "I'll tell you later. I'm hungry right now. Maybe if we're lucky, there might be some of Huldah's bread left."

The boys found Shammah and Abinadab sitting together sharpening their swords in between eating handfuls of the parched grain David's father had sent. When they saw David, they jumped up and ran to meet him.

"It's not true, is it!" Shammah protested. "The king isn't really going to let you fight Goliath, is he?"

Abinadab pointed at David and shook his finger. "It'd better not be true! Have you any idea how stupid the whole thing sounds! Can you imagine how worried Father and Mother would be if they knew you were even thinking about fighting that giant?"

Joab's mouth dropped open. He looked first at David and then at David's brothers.

David ignored them all and helped himself to a handful of parched grain. He sat down, leaned against a bedroll, and began munching the grain.

"Are you really that worried about Father and Mother? And to be honest, are you the least bit worried about me? Actually, I suspect the two of you and Eliab are probably more worried about yourselves than anyone else." David popped a few more grains into his open mouth. "I can't say that I blame you, I guess. I'd be worried about becoming a slave to the Philistines, too."

"Then why are you even thinking about going out there to fight the giant?" Abinadab had his hands on his hips now. "You'll be committing suicide for sure! You don't stand a chance, David!" Abinadab was almost shouting now.

David looked at Abinadab and Shammah, and then over his shoulder at the Philistine camp. "I don't mean to be disrespectful," he said solemnly, "but you two are forgetting one very important thing. If God is for us, who can be against us?"

"You're not going to use that old line on us this time! How do you even know it is God's will that you fight Goliath? Did God Himself tell you to fight the giant?" Shammah asked sarcastically.

David stood to his feet and looked Shammah straight in the eye. "Anyone who has the nerve to curse our God and say that He is weak or even dead needs to be taught otherwise. The giant says we will be his slaves one day, and I'm afraid we will—unless," David paused and then added, "unless we can fight him and win! Then, and only then, by God's goodness will we be free at last from these horrible wars with the Philistines."

Shammah and Abinadab just stood staring at David.

David pointed to heaven. "My loyalty to the living God is greater than my fear of Goliath, and that is exactly why I will fight the giant today. Not because I want to die, but because I want God's name to live."

"Suit yourself." It was Eliab. How long he had been listening to the conversation, David couldn't tell, but he realized that it didn't really matter.

"When Father has to come down here and take your body back to Bethlehem to have you buried, those words will sound good at your funeral—but that's all the good they are going to do you." Eliab sat down on the ground as he helped himself to the last loaf of Huldah's homemade bread.

"That's the difference between you and me, Eliab." David tried to speak calmly. "I happen to think that God wants us to win the battle with Goliath. You don't."

"That's not true!" Eliab protested between mouthfuls of the bread.

"Yes it is. If you really believed that God would help us win, then you'd offer to fight Goliath yourself."

"There you go again!" Eliab's eyes flashed. "You always think you're better than we are, just because you *think* your view of God is different from ours doesn't mean you are better!"

"We *will* win the battle today against Goliath," David added, "and when Goliath is dead, you will know that the Lord's arm is not weak. At that point, you will believe it is true—but not until then."

David turned and walked away. What was the use? It was hard being respectful when his brothers put him down. David didn't want to argue about God. What was there to argue about? God existed and there was no other being anywhere like Him. No one could stand before His power, so why argue about what He could or couldn't do? It seemed silly to even try.

*   *   *

It was late in the afternoon when the ominous rumbling of Goliath's challenge cut through the hot afternoon air. David could hear it clear back inside the command post. A priest placed his hand on David's head and asked God's blessing on him, and then King Saul and his royal guard walked with David from the military command post on down to the front lines.

Joab and Abishai hurried to keep up with the group. Everything was happening so fast. David turned to catch one last glimpse of his friends. They looked frightened, but there was no time for David to reassure them.

No one else spoke to David either. What was the point? Everything had already been said. David passed through the main detachment of soldiers. He passed his own brothers standing ready with their swords drawn. And then he passed the best of the king's forces, who were on the very front lines.

As David drew near to the Philistine front lines, he could see Goliath standing across the ravine to the west. The giant was carrying a huge spear! David nearly gasped. It looked like one of the gigantic metal bars that David had seen stonecutters use to pry rocks loose at the quarries. Judging by the height of the soldiers standing around Goliath, the spear had to be longer than David was tall!

And the giant had a sword strapped to his side. David shuddered. He didn't even want to think about how heavy and sharp it must be! The giant could probably cut down a tree with it!

David's mouth nearly dropped open as he saw the heavy metal armor that hung down across Goliath's chest. It had scores of metal plates sewn together like scales on a fish. *Whoa!* If David ever had to wear that piece of armor, he just knew he'd fall to the ground and never get up! It had to weigh a lot! Probably as much as David himself.

But it was Goliath's huge helmet that held David's attention. It made the giant look even taller with its red feathers sticking out of the top.

And standing out in front of Goliath was another soldier carrying a shield. David knew an armor bearer had to be strong to carry a shield big enough to protect the giant's body, but even so, the armor bearer looked like a dwarf beside the giant.

David looked around and realized that he was standing by himself at the edge of the rocky ravine. He had walked the rest of the way by himself, and suddenly he felt very much alone. "Help me, God!" was all he could whisper. "Help me to be brave for You!"

And then David heard the giant's voice. Somehow David had managed to tune out the deepness of the huge voice while he had been walking steadily toward it. Or had the giant been speaking at all? David wasn't sure, but he wondered, *Does the giant realize that I'm the one who is going to fight him?*

"King Saul! Send out your fiercest warrior to fight me!" Goliath bellowed. "By the power of Dagon and all the gods of the Philistines, I challenge you!" He paused and then almost as an afterthought, he added, "If your God is alive and can hear us today, I challenge you to fight for Him and His honor!"

David jumped down over the steep bank of the rocky ravine between the two armies. He set his jaw in determination for the second time that day. This was it! This was the final signal he needed from God. Goliath, of course, had not thought that he might be uttering his own death sentence, but David knew that he had. If there was any challenge that an Israelite had a hard time ignoring, it was a challenge to honor the Lord God of hosts. David would answer that challenge here today, just as the giant had asked.

An afternoon breeze ruffled David's dark hair as he reached down to the bed of the ravine and picked up five smooth stones. He needed to choose them quickly, but carefully—stones about half the size of his fist would work best in this situation. David put them into his shepherd's pouch, one stone for each of the five Philistine cities that had been making war against the Israelite people for so long now—Ashdod, Gath, Ekron, Ashkelon, and Gaza. One, two, three, four, five. The stones David chose must be perfect, as round as possible, and smooth with no rough edges to catch on the leather strands of his sling.

And then David was looking up into the face of the giant towering above him at the edge of the ravine. From this angle, the giant Goliath looked even taller and even more frightening.

It was almost as if the giant were standing on top of a city wall. David swallowed hard. *How am I ever going to get up over the edge of the ravine to fight the giant? And when I get there, how will my stones and sling ever make a dent in his armor, let alone bring him down?*

For an instant David wished that he were back with his sheep where it was quiet and peaceful. For an instant he almost wished he were back where the wind whistled over the hills and the turtledoves cooed their late-afternoon calls. But only for an instant.

David sent another silent prayer to heaven and took a deep breath. *Stay calm,* he reminded himself. *God will provide a way. He always does.*

THE BATTLE BELONGS TO THE LORD

And now Goliath was shouting again. It was as if the giant was just now realizing that David intended to fight him. "What is this?" he roared. "A boy!"

Goliath looked across the ravine at the Israelite army. He scanned the crowd for Israel's king. "King Saul!" he bellowed. "I've never been more insulted in all my life! You must think I'm a dog, or you wouldn't be sending a boy to fight me! Look at him! He's carrying a stick!"

Goliath began to curse and swear. He shoved his armor bearer aside, and the huge shield clanged to the ground. As Goliath ranted and raved, the veins on his neck began to bulge, and his face turned purple with rage.

The giant's sudden anger took David by surprise, and he almost stumbled backward. David didn't know what he should have expected—scorn and mocking perhaps, but not anger! The giant—only twenty to thirty paces away—was raving like a madman. David found himself wanting to turn around and scramble back up the way he had come, but his feet felt glued to the ground.

David was sure he could feel the giant's hot breath as he snarled and growled like some wild animal. The sun glistened off the shiny plates of armor as Goliath gripped his spear first with one hand and then the other. It was as if Goliath was in a hurry to get at David, but somehow couldn't.

The late afternoon was warm, and sweat was dripping from

beneath Goliath's metal helmet, causing the helmet to slide forward. Now and then he put his hand to his face to wipe the sweat away. Was Goliath frightened? Could he possibly be worried about this fight with a shepherd boy? The idea seemed ridiculous, and yet something in Goliath's face made David think it might be so.

David slipped his hand into his shepherd's pouch and ran his fingers over the smooth stones, counting them one by one. To him the stones were like his best friends. For hours on end he had practiced with his sling, and always he had taken the time to choose the stones he needed. Each battle was different—the lions, the bears, the wolves, and the bandits. Each had required a different kind of stone for the job at hand; each had required a different kind of courage from the boy. And today was no different. Today, these stones would help him have the courage to do what he knew he had to do.

"Well, what are you waiting for!" Goliath roared. He shook his head like a wild beast. "Get up here, boy! Let's get this over with! There are plenty of wild animals in these hills that would like some supper! When we're done here, I'm going to serve you to them on a silver platter!"

Every eye in the Israelite army strained to see David as he drew himself up to his full height. "I'm not afraid of you, Goliath! You talk big about your sword and spear and shield, but I'm coming to you today with more powerful weapons than you can possibly imagine!"

David's voice rang out among the hills overlooking the ravine. "Today I come to you in the name of the God of Israel. He is Captain of the hosts of heaven and earth." David lifted his arm and pointed at Goliath, "Today Israel's God will deliver you into my hand, Goliath. But it isn't my strength or skill that will win this battle. It's God's, and today everyone on this battlefield will know that there is a God in Israel! Today everyone will know that

God does not save with swords and spears, but by faith in the power of His name!"

Not a soldier spoke as Goliath and David faced each other in the late-afternoon sunlight. To David it seemed as if time were standing still for this showdown between good and evil—but in an instant the moment had passed.

Goliath slapped his helmet to push it back up over his forehead and out of his eyes. "All right!" he roared. "If you're not going to come up here, then I'm going to come down there!"

The giant jerked his sword from its sheath and began to run toward David! The largest stone was already in David's sling. The sling was going round and round as the giant charged toward the edge of the ravine. To David it seemed as if everything were moving in slow motion—the giant, the sling, and the stone that was now flying through the air toward its mark! In the split second before the stone hit the giant square in the forehead, Goliath saw it coming, but was too late! There was no time for him to duck or swerve. With a sickening thud, it crashed into his skull, knocking him senseless. The giant's huge body staggered and stumbled, but his momentum kept him coming until he toppled down into the rocky gorge. His body came to rest at David's feet, out of sight from the soldiers on either side of the ravine!

Goliath's huge body lay on the ground in front of David, silent at last. *Is it over? Is the giant dead?* David wondered. It had all happened so fast!

After a few moments of stunned silence, both Israelite and Philistine soldiers were rushing to the ravine to stare down at Goliath, now face down in the dirt. David, realizing the opportunity of the moment, ran forward and pulled Goliath's huge sword from its sheath. He lifted it high in the air and shouted a battle cry of victory. "The sword of the Lord and of Israel!"

The Philistine soldiers looked at one another and then at the

Israelite soldiers across the ravine. Instantly they realized that their worst nightmare had come true! Goliath, their champion of champions, the giant who had won so many victories for them in battle, was dead!

"The victory is ours!" David's voice again split the afternoon air like a thunderbolt. He pointed at the Philistine army and shouted, "To your own country, you miserable Philistines!"

Immediately the Israelite army was flowing down into the ravine like a summer flash flood. They filled it and spilled over its edge as they climbed out on the other side. Energized with all the anger and fear from forty days of waiting, the Israelite soldiers chased the Philistine army up and over the hills toward the west.

NATIONAL HERO

Twilight had settled over the landscape when David and the Israelite men of war returned from chasing the Philistine army. The men were tired, but their eyes shone with the excitement of victory. Even Joab and Abishai had joined in on the chase.

When David and the Israelite soldiers came through the ravine on their way back to camp, they stopped at the spot where David had met Goliath. Everyone could still see the imprint in the dirt where Goliath had fallen.

"Wow! What a day!" Abishai said excitedly. "You took that giant down, David!"

"He sure did!" Joab replied.

"The Lord and I did." David grinned at Abishai.

Abishai nodded his head. "Yeah, you're right, but He asked you to help Him out!"

Joab looked at David proudly. "You know, David, Abishai is right. You're the hero here today."

Scores of soldiers stopped in the ravine to congratulate David too. "Joab's right!" several shouted. "You are the hero, David, and we owe our lives to you!" David tried to protest, but soon hundreds of soldiers were repeating the line, and then they were carrying him back to camp on their shoulders. They paraded him all around and up and down among the rows of tents, until they came to the army's command post at the rear of the camp.

King Saul was smiling like David had never seen him smile before. The soldiers cheered and slapped David on the back and told him what a great job he'd done. And right there among them all was Shammah, Abinadab, and Eliab.

Eliab smiled at David and then reached out and hugged him. "I'm proud of you, David! Father will be proud of you too." Eliab hung his head a bit. "You're a hero, David, and you deserve to be one. I'm sorry I doubted you and gave you such a hard time."

David was nearly bursting with happiness. To win the king's favor was important, but to win Eliab's respect was even more special. All his life David had wanted to be somebody in Eliab's eyes, and now in one short afternoon, it had happened. David had been able to honor God and serve his country and king, but growing ten feet tall in the eyes of his brother Eliab was the best part of all!

And now the king was preparing to speak. The officers had brought out his makeshift throne, and the king was wearing his royal robes. A crown had been placed on the king's head, making the ceremony even more official.

"Valiant men of war!" the king spoke loudly so that everyone could hear. "This is a great day in Israel! We have been blessed beyond our wildest hopes, and God has been good to us! Not since the early days of my reign do I remember such rejoicing among the people, and many in Israel have yet to hear the good news! Goliath, our greatest enemy, is dead! Today Israel has experienced victory at the hand of a boy, but not just an ordinary boy."

The king beckoned for David to come near his throne. He laid his hand on David's shoulder. "I first learned of this boy's talents when he came to my court. He plays the lyre—and he plays it well! I have not heard a better musician, and I am hoping that we can get him to play for us all during our celebration here this evening!"

The king smiled. "But I understand that David is skilled in other ways, too! Here before you is a shepherd boy who can fight like a warrior among his father's sheep! He makes war on wild beasts of the wilderness! Lions—bears—wolves, and he even fights bandits who would steal his sheep! And how does he do all this? With a sling! And it is his sling that has brought us a victory today!"

The king stood to his feet and gave David a little bow. David gasped as he realized the significance of what the king had done. The king might bow before a priest at the holy sanctuary or before a prophet of the Lord—but never before a common person. And the king had just bowed before a shepherd boy!

David wondered for just a moment whether the king knew about the anointing ceremony in Bethlehem on the night of the sacrificial feast. It didn't seem likely. But could it be the king was beginning to see that David had many talents, and that these talents would make him a great leader among his people? The thought of such a thing was a bit frightening.

David remembered the days of playing for King Saul at his royal fortress in Gibeah. *If the king can fly into fits of rage over a spilled cup of wine, what might he say about my anointing? What might he do if he thought that I might one day be the next king of Israel instead of his own son?* David didn't want to think about that. He knew he must not think such thoughts. It just wasn't safe. Even though David had killed Goliath, the greatest enemy of Israel, Saul was still king, and that gave him almost unlimited power.

"Have you anything to say to the men, my boy?" The king was looking at David affectionately, as if David were his own son.

David faced the crowd of Israelite soldiers. There were thousands of them crowed into this little valley, but David looked for the familiar faces among them. There were Eliab, Abinadab, and Shammah standing with their arms folded proudly across their chests. David could see his best friends, Joab and Abishai, and the other boys from Bethlehem. And Abner was there. The old general looked kinder now. His face did not look chiseled in stone as it had when David first met him.

"I don't really know what to say," David began. "I'm glad that I was here today to help my people. Israel is a great nation. We have been given this wonderful land of milk and honey, and I'm glad we've been able to convince the Philistines to give us some of it back today!"

The crowd of soldiers burst into laughter at David's comment, and he smiled sheepishly.

"I hope that we can all learn some lessons here today," David continued. "Me? I want to learn that God can help anyone gain the victory—even me, no matter how small or unimportant I might think I am." David grinned and ran his fingers slowly through his hair. "And for the rest of you, I think it's important to remember that we should never give up. If you just have faith in God, small as it may seem, God can do amazing things. He can do a miracle for you, and He will, if you ask Him." David paused and then grinned again. "That's all for now, I guess."

The crowd of soldiers burst into cheers, and the king stepped forward to put his arm around David's shoulders. The men cheered for what seemed an eternity, and then someone brought David a lyre.

"And now, men," the king shouted, "I think it's time we do some celebrating, and who better to lead us than David, the shepherd warrior!"

As the cheering continued, David was escorted to the center of camp. By the light of a hundred burning campfires, he and the other musicians struck up a familiar tune, and soon there was laughing and clapping and dancing. The men joined arms and circled the fires, turning in one direction and then the other, as they kept time with the music. Their praises to God lifted higher and higher in the night sky like the sparks from the cheerful fires all around them.

And there was food too. News had spread quickly about David's great victory, and soon farmers were coming into the camp, their wagons and carts and donkeys loaded with food. There were stacks of barley loaves, pots of bubbling stew, piles of round cheeses, and baskets of dried fruit. And several bullocks had been brought, so the meat was soon roasting on spits over large open fires. David had never before seen so much food at one time.

When it was late and David couldn't stay awake any longer, he found a secluded place at the edge of camp and lay down for the night. He could still hear the music of the tambourines, flutes, and lyres, but that was all right. He was glad that everyone else was having fun. He was tired, so he knew he'd be able to sleep anyway, no matter how much commotion there was.

"What a day for Israel," David smiled up at the stars as he rolled himself up in his mantle. "And what a day for the God of heaven and earth! Thank You, Lord, for everything," David whispered. "The Lord of heaven's armies is here among us; the God of Israel is our fortress."

David stared into the darkness and let out a tired sigh. The goose bumps raced across his body as he realized how much he had been through since early morning. He was tired from his long walk from Bethlehem. He was weary from the long afternoon of nervously waiting to fight Goliath. He was worn out from the battle and from chasing the Philistines out of the hill country of Judea. But more than anything else, David was exhausted from having to listen to everyone congratulate him, the shepherd boy, now Israel's latest hero. It was as if everyone wanted to be near him, to ask him how he had had the courage to face the giant. They kept asking him about the look on Goliath's face at having to fight a boy and what exactly David had done to kill the giant. It was like they enjoyed it too much, as if they loved to hate the Philistines.

David had grown tired of sharing the details, and he didn't like hearing everyone gloat over the death of their enemies. David couldn't really blame them, but as Israelites, why couldn't they just be glad that they were safe without taking great delight in the fact that someone had had to die, even if it was Goliath?

Not that David wasn't glad the giant was gone—he was! David could still see Goliath clearly in his mind, towering above him on the edge of that ravine. He was glad that he would never have to face that giant again! But hate! David didn't like having feelings of hate. His mother's words of advice kept coming back to him. Words David had heard her say many times. "Hate is not a good thing, even if it's toward the Philistines. It's like a slow poison eating away at your heart."

And she was right. With hate in the world, there would always be war somewhere. There would always be pain and suffering and senseless battles in which thousands died in a single day. David tried not to think about any of that. Maybe someday God would bring peace to the land so that there would be no more hate.

David closed his eyes. For now he was just grateful that his battle with Goliath was over. For now he just wanted to sleep after a very long day.

HOMECOMING

Fluffy white clouds scudded across the blue sky of what promised to be yet another perfect day. David was eager to be up and on his way with Joab and Abishai, but first he had to do the proper thing. The king had invited David to eat the morning meal with him.

As he sat down in the king's quarters, David's eyes feasted on the food that was spread out before him. It looked as if great pains had been taken to find the best of the land for the table of the king. The first of the season's early grapes and olives had been brought in for the meal. There were dried figs and raisins, a dish of cucumbers, leeks, and chickpeas, and a stew that smelled of onions and lentils. There were several kinds of bread and sweet cakes, too, and sitting right in the middle of the table was a platter of leftover meat from the night before.

David had seen food like this at the king's court in Gibeah. However, he was surprised that so much food could show up in so short a time at a battlefield. Probably the victory over the Philistines the day before had had something to do with that.

David turned down the roast beef—he preferred simpler food, especially so early in the morning. However, he did take several helpings of chickpeas and lentil stew, and then grabbed a cake of raisins to finish off his meal.

"David, my boy," the king asked, "what would you think of staying on at the fortress as part of my bodyguard?" The king looked intently at David. His eyes searched the face of the brave young shepherd boy. "I would be willing to pay you a wage, of course, but money is no object, my son." The king continued, "After what happened on the battlefield yesterday, I simply must have you at my court—for good luck, if for no other reason."

David sat listening to the king talk, and he knew what his answer had to be. He knew he couldn't turn down the king's offer—it would be unthinkable! And besides, the king was not really asking David to stay, he was commanding him to.

"So, what do you say, my boy?" The king was waiting for an answer, and David knew he couldn't make him wait long.

"I would be happy to serve my king," David replied. "However, I would like to ask that the court allow me to go home to see my family for a few days."

And so it was that David left for Bethlehem with his brothers and the other soldiers who lived in that part of Judea. The king, his bodyguard, and three thousand troops headed for the fortress at Gibeah, while the rest of the army disbanded and went home.

Joab, Abishai, and David did their best to keep up with the other soldiers, but it was difficult.

Abishai finally shouted at his donkey, "Come on, Buz! You're the slowest animal this side of the Jordan!" He lightly prodded the stubborn donkey with a stick. "I don't suppose it matters to you that we started out at the front of this pack train! For all you care, you'd just as soon finish last!"

David wheezed and then sneezed several times as they followed the slowly moving procession of soldiers and pack animals. "These clouds of dust are going to choke the life out of me—I think I've breathed in enough of this stuff to plant a garden!"

"Come on, boys!" laughed Joab. "You two sound like old men! We've got a party waiting for us back home in Bethlehem! I can hardly wait to see what kind of a hero's welcome you're going to get, David! Probably every girl in town is going to want to see you!"

"And one in particular," chimed Abishai.

"What are you talking about?" David retorted, but secretly he didn't really mind their teasing. At least not about Abi.

It was late afternoon when the returning soldiers and boys neared Bethlehem, and a shout went up from the town's people as the village watchmen caught sight of them. Word spread quickly, and before they had even arrived at the village gate, a procession of girls came running out to meet them. The girls danced down the roadway to the music of flutes and jingling tambourines. Abi was with them, and David thought that there probably wasn't a prettier girl in all of Israel.

The girls sang with excitement, their words bringing new life to the sleepy village of Bethlehem. The words echoed off the surrounding hillsides near Bethlehem adding to the joy of the celebration. The rest of the village came out to meet them, too, and soon everyone was talking at once. David's brothers told the villagers everything, and Jesse's pride was obvious. However, the crowd grew quiet when David's mother arrived on the scene.

"David, I don't know what to say." She wiped a tear from her eye. "You rascal! If I had known you would offer to fight the biggest giant in the land, I wouldn't have let you go, even if I thought you could win!" She smiled faintly before admitting, "I suppose it all turned out for the best in the end."

The celebration moved to the threshing floor on the outskirts of Bethlehem. The threshing floor was large enough to include all the people who would be arriving from surrounding villages as the evening wore on.

And what a celebration it was as darkness settled over the village and campfires were lighted! There was joyful dancing and speeches and lots of food—David thought he had seen enough food already in one day to last him a lifetime. After the victory against the Philistines the day before, there had been the feast in the Israelite camp after dark. Then there had been the huge meal he had eaten with the king just that morning, and now, of course, there was another celebration meal.

So much had happened in so short a time. It was certainly going to be a week to remember for years to come.

Someone brought out David's lyre, and soon a band of musicians was playing to the clapping of hands and stomping of feet. David moved around among the musicians and encouraged them all as they played one song after another in praise to the God of heaven. "I will sing of the Lord's unfailing love forever, I will sing! I will sing!" The chords of the songs rose on the evening air like the warmth of the campfires.

Somewhere during the night David drifted away from all the noise and laughter and found Joab and Abishai. They were standing by a campfire near an old watchtower overlooking the Valley of Rephaim. Not surprisingly, they were having target practice with their slings by the light of the campfire.

Joab glanced at David as he put a stone into his sling and sent it flying off into the night. "Well, David, I guess it's safe to say that things will never be the same again for you around here!" *Crack!* The stone went through a window opening in the watchtower and hit the wall inside.

"You think so?" David handed Joab another stone.

"Come on, David!" Joab gave Abishai a wink. "You know very well what I'm talking about! So much has happened in the last few months, and things are probably going to change for you a lot more too. You're not just a shepherd boy anymore, David. You've been places, and done things." Joab stopped swinging his sling. "You've played your music for the king in his royal court. You've been to a major battlefield, David, and you've fought a giant and beat him! You killed a giant, David!" Joab started laughing. "I think that's definitely going to get everybody's attention! Everybody who knows you, likes you, David, and now, get this, Abishai! I hear that the king wants David to come and stay with him at the court for good—for always. To be part of his permanent bodyguard."

"Noooo!" Abishai dropped the stone he was getting ready to put in his sling.

"I heard the rumor too," a voice came from the darkness, "and I'm not surprised. I guess I should have thought something like this would happen."

David turned to look into the shadows behind him. It was Abi. She had come out of the darkness like a cat on velvet feet.

"Abi," was all he could say.

"When you become rich and famous, you won't forget about us here in little old Bethlehem, will you, David?" Her voice was so soft that David could hardly hear it.

"I could never forget you, Abi. Or you, either, Joab and Abishai. You three are my friends! My best friends! Whatever I do, and wherever I go, there will always be a place for you near me." David wanted to tell the boys about the secret meeting with the prophet, but he knew that it still wasn't safe to do that, and the look in Abi's eyes reminded David of his need for silence.

Abi put another piece of wood on the campfire. "The Lord is with you, David. You have proven that to us and to all of Israel." She got a faraway look on her face. "Bethlehem is such a small town," she added as she stared into the fire, "but I think great things are going to come out of this place."

Joab stirred the fire with a stick, sending sparks flying up into the night sky. "David, you're from Bethlehem. Maybe you'll be a great person some day."

Abishai nodded his head. "He will—I know he will. How could he not be great! Look at all he's done already!"

David didn't know what to say. What could he say? He didn't feel as if he deserved the praise his friends were giving him. Of course he was glad for all the adventures he'd had. He had learned to fight lions and bears as a shepherd, but it had made him learn to trust God more. He had felt honored at being asked to play for the king in his court, and being at the right place at the right time to fight Goliath had been a chance of a lifetime. And then there was the special anointing ceremony that night in Bethlehem. David was a little frightened at the thought of what the anointing might mean. To be anointed meant one was being set aside for a very special job. David wasn't sure he was really ready to be someone important. Would he grow proud? Would he forget God as King Saul had done? By God's grace he hoped not.

"Hey!" David finally found his tongue. "God is the One who is great! We owe Him everything! Someday He will send a Savior to this world to save us from our sins!"

"He's right!" Abi looked thoughtful. "God is good. I wonder, do you think that when the Messiah comes, He will be born in a small village like Bethlehem?"

"Hey!" Joab laughed. "That's a neat idea! Who knows! Maybe He'll even be related to one of us."

"You never can tell," David said. "With God, all things are possible."

David glanced over at the villagers celebrating on the threshing floor, and suddenly it dawned on him that things really had changed for him. He didn't feel like just a little shepherd boy anymore. He didn't feel unimportant, like someone that has to do all the leftover jobs no one else wants to do. Instead, he felt like a man. After all, he had done a man's job. The truth was, no man had even had the courage to do what David had done—to face a giant in the name of the Lord, and then win. And to think that the soldiers in the Israelite camp the day before had tried to convince him that he was a troublemaker.

David grew thoughtful. From shepherd boy to giant killer, and then someday maybe even king—that was quite a leap, but it didn't matter. He wasn't afraid. With God on his side, he knew he could do anything God asked him to do.

CPSIA information can be obtained
at www.ICGtesting.com
Printed in the USA
FFHW011933120819
54163756-59877FF